Sarah

Also by Mary Christner Borntrager in Large Print:

Andy
Annie
Daniel
Ellie
Rachel
Rebecca
Reuben

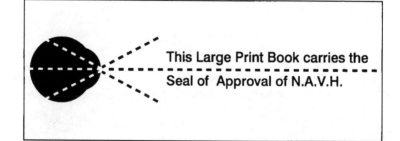

This Large Print Book carries the Seal of Approval of N.A.V.H.

Sarah

Mary Christner Borntrager

Thorndike Press • Waterville, Maine

Published in 2002 by arrangement with Herald Press,
a division of Mennonite Publishing, Inc.

Thorndike Press Large Print Christian Fiction Series.

The tree indicium is a trademark of Thorndike Press.

The text of this Large Print edition is unabridged.
Other aspects of the book may vary from the original edition.

Cover design by Thorndike Press Staff.

Set in 16 pt. Plantin by Elena Picard.

Printed in the United States on permanent paper.

Library of Congress Cataloging-in-Publication Data

Borntrager, Mary Christner, 1921–
    Sarah / Mary Christner Borntrager.
      p. cm.
    ISBN 0-7862-4526-3 (lg. print : hc : alk. paper)
    1. Amish — Fiction. 2. Large type books. I. Title.
PS3552.O7544 S27 2002
   813'.54—dc21
                                    2002071990

To Loretta,
who has been
such an inspiration

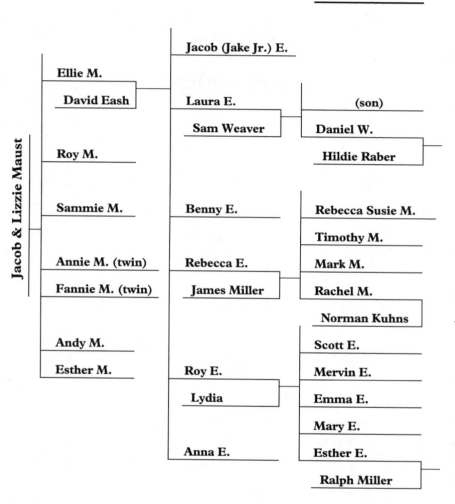

Jacob & Lizzie Maust

Ellie M.
David Eash

Roy M.

Sammie M.

Annie M. (twin)
Fannie M. (twin)

Andy M.
Esther M.

Jacob (Jake Jr.) E.

Laura E.
Sam Weaver

Benny E.

Rebecca E.
James Miller

Roy E.
Lydia

Anna E.

(son)
Daniel W.
Hildie Raber

Rebecca Susie M.
Timothy M.
Mark M.
Rachel M.

Norman Kuhns
Scott E.
Mervin E.
Emma E.
Mary E.
Esther E.
Ralph Miller

Christina Maria W.

Eli W.

Reuben W.

Henry T.

Salome W.

Joe T.

Adam W.

Levi W.

Lucy

Jonas W.

Sarah T.

Mandy W.

Mahlon Mast

Samuel Troyer

Edna T.

Lizzie May W.

Lisabet T.

Hannah W.

Lloyd Schrock

Susan S.

Frieda S.

Roseann (Rosie) W.

Ruth S.

Barbara S.

Polly M.

Esther S.

Ben M.

Mandy S.

Sara M.

Lloyd S.

Levi M.

Jonas S.

Effie M.

William M.

Contents

1

Forever Eleven

"Quit *suddling* (splashing) around in the dishwater and get those dishes washed. You'll be late for school again."

Sarah Troyer began washing as fast as she could. She wished her mother were well. Then they need not have a *Maut* (hired girl).

Her mother, Mandy, had been ill now for several months so her father, Samuel, hired Sadie Zook to help out. Sadie tried to be a good worker, but she was often short with the children.

Sarah's younger sister, Edna, was drying the dishes. She was not quite six and had to stand on a stool to reach the countertop.

"I wish I were older. Then we wouldn't need a Maut," Sarah whispered to Edna. "*Ich duht die Arwet selwer zu* (I'd do the work myself, too)."

"*Was hoscht yuscht du saagt* (just what

did you say)?" asked Sadie.

Sarah was afraid to answer.

"You'd better be careful what you say. My ears are pretty sharp. All right, if you won't tell me, then maybe Edna will."

Edna began to cry.

"*Ach, so ferdarewe die Kinner* (oh, such spoiled children)," Sadie complained, giving Sarah a push away from the sink.

"Now look how you got the floor all wet with your *suddling*," scolded Sadie. "Dry your hands and get your lunch pail. The boys are halfway down the lane already. You know you aren't supposed to walk alone. *Geh mol* (go once)!"

Sarah was glad to leave. She liked school. But she felt sorry for her younger sister, Edna, and the *Buppeli* Lisabet (baby Elizabeth). They had to be in Sadie's company all day. At least Sarah could escape for a little while.

"*Waard* (wait)!" she called to her brothers. She was tying her bonnet as she ran. In her haste she dropped her lunch. The lid of her pail opened, spilling her egg sandwich, cold sausage, and half-moon pie on the ground. Her brothers came to her aid.

"Here," offered Joe, who was twelve, a year older than Sarah, "I'll help you."

"My half-moon pie is all *verdutzt* (ruined)," Sarah lamented.

"Don't worry." Her big brother comforted her. "I'll trade lunches with you."

"But then you won't have enough to eat!" Sarah exclaimed.

"I'll have what I need to get by on. We're family and must stick together. Isn't that what Dad told us, since Mom is sick?"

"*Yah* (yes)," Sarah answered gratefully, "but I dropped the pail, and so I'll take my own."

"Here, then," offered Joe, as he opened his own lunch. "Take my pie. I don't eat as much as Henry does. Really, *ich geb nix drum* (I don't care)."

"Well, all right," Sarah consented and added, "*Danki* (thanks)."

"We must hurry or teacher will mark us tardy," Henry reminded them. He was thirteen, the oldest, and felt his responsibility.

"Yah, and if we're marked tardy three times, we lose three recesses." Joe didn't want that to happen.

This seemed to lend wings to their feet as they hurried toward the little red schoolhouse. Rounding the last bend in the road, they were happy to see the Byler and Lapp children making their way to school.

"They're never tardy," Henry commented. "So we must be on time."

Inside, the one-room school was cheerful and friendly. Bright pictures covered the spaces above the chalkboards. The warm, happy smiles of Miss Kinsinger and the children were a welcome sight. It had a calming effect upon Sarah's troubled heart.

"Will you be my *Botching* partner at recess?" asked her friend Katie Kuhns. *Botching* was played much like peas-porridge-hot. Two girls would sit opposite each other and clap their hands together as they said a silly rhyme.

Sarah was pleased. She liked Katie a lot.

"Yah, I will," Sarah answered.

"Sit with me at lunchtime, too," Katie invited her.

"Oh, I'd like to, Katie," Sarah responded, "but I promised Lydia yesterday already I'd eat with her."

"Can't you tell her you'll eat with her another day?" begged her little friend.

"*Ach* (oh), I'd better not. She might get mad at me."

"All right, children, everyone go to your seat and settle down. It's time to begin," Miss Kinsinger called out.

There was a shuffle of feet along with

oh's and ah's as the pupils found their places.

"This morning I've asked Regina to lead our singing. Please take out your songbooks."

Most of the songbooks were already lying on top of each desk because this was always the way the school began. Regina walked to the front of the room. She was in the eighth grade and, in Sarah's eyes, the prettiest girl in all the school. Of course, some said she was too fancy for Amish and that her parents should be more strict. Sarah even wished she had been named Regina. It sounded so poetic. Sarah Regina — yes, that name would be fine. She would like that much better than just plain *Sarah*.

So lost had she been in her thoughts that she didn't hear the page number announced. Everyone else began to sing "*Gott des Himmels und der Erden* (God of heaven and of earth)." Sarah had no idea what page to look for. She stretched to see the book of the child in front of her. Perhaps she might be able to make out the number.

To her surprise and dismay, Miss Kinsinger stood by her desk, closed Sarah's book, and led her to the front of the room. There she placed Sarah in a corner with her face to the wall. Tears filled Sarah's eyes and splashed on her dark blue apron, leaving ugly marks.

"You will learn to pay attention," Miss Kinsinger whispered as the singing went on.

Sarah's face burned with shame. She had not meant to do anything wrong. Now Katie Kuhns may not want her for a *Botching* partner in first recess or for eating together at noon. Why did her day start out so badly?

After the singing exercises, Miss Kinsinger read a Bible story and had the children recite Bible verses in German. Then Sarah was allowed to return to her seat. She didn't look up but walked with her head bowed, feeling sorry and ashamed. Her brothers pitied her and wanted to comfort her in some way.

At recess big brother Henry soothed her. "You didn't mean to do wrong. I just know you didn't." That helped Sarah a great deal.

Soon Katie came out the door and asked, "Sarah, are you ready to be my partner?"

That helped still more. Maybe the day wasn't so bad after all.

While eating lunch, Sarah told Katie

about her accident with her lunch pail. They both laughed about it.

Before long, Sarah told Katie about her wish for a new name.

"Oh, I think Sarah Regina would be a pretty name for you. I'll call you that if you want me to," said Katie.

Her friend's response gave Sarah a wonderful feeling.

"I'm going to ask my mother and father if they will give me that name," Sarah declared.

Then she remembered. *Mother is sick and the Maut said not to bother Mom with unnecessary things. If only we wouldn't need a Maut. But I think I shall be eleven forever!*

2

Not Like Mom's!

There was one thing about the *Maut* (hired girl) that Sarah couldn't understand. She decided to discuss it with her brothers on the way home from school.

"Do you boys ever notice how *gut* (good) Sadie is to us when Dad's around?" she asked.

"*Yah* (yes)," Henry answered, "but I'm not around her as much as you are."

"Why do you suppose she's so snappy when Dad isn't close by?" Sarah asked.

"Maybe she wants to act like *Mamm* (Mother)," Joe replied.

"Our mother never acts like she does," Sarah objected. "She would never *ziehe* (pull) our ears or snap at us. I almost hate to go home anymore."

"*Ach* (oh), Sarah, don't say that!" Henry exclaimed. "Think of Edna and the *Buppeli* (baby). Wouldn't you miss them? They have to be with Sadie all day."

"I know," Sarah replied. "Oh, if only Mom wasn't sick. She isn't coughing so much anymore. Maybe she'll get better soon. Then we won't need Sadie anymore."

"Come on, let's catch up with the Bylers," Henry urged. "Raymond said something happened at their place yesterday, and he was going to tell me after school."

It was always fun being with the Byler children. Regina was one of that family, and Sarah gladly walked with her.

"Hey, you slowpokes," Raymond called. "Hurry up, or I can't tell you about our surprise."

"Okay, what is it?" Henry asked as they caught up with their friends.

"You won't believe this." Raymond loved to keep them in suspense.

"Well, what is it? Come on, tell us," Joe begged.

"*Ach, der Raymond will yuscht zaerte* (oh, Raymond just wants to tease)," Regina griped. "If he doesn't quit, I'll tell you."

"No, you don't," Raymond warned his sister. "I was ready to tell. One of our cows had twin calves yesterday morning, and one of our mares had twin colts. But the best surprise — Dad promised that if I help with the work real good this summer, one of those colts is mine. I said I'd help extra good. My mind isn't made up yet which one to pick. They are both fine colts."

"That is all we will hear around our place is *Hutchli, Hutchli, Hutchli* (colt, colt, colt)," Regina predicted.

"Boy, I wish *my* dad would give me a colt to raise," Henry said wistfully. "I'd take care of it fine."

"Me, too," Joe agreed.

"What were you talking about when you came out of the schoolhouse?" Regina asked. "Usually you're ahead of most of the walkers. It must have been important since it took so long for you to catch up to us."

"Oh, that," snorted Joe. "Maybe it wasn't anything in particular." Now *he* was trying to tease and make the Byler children curious. Or perhaps he was embarrassed to tell.

"Come on," Regina insisted. "We told *you*."

"Yeah, but this is different," Henry explained.

"That doesn't matter. *Raus mit* (out with it)!"

"We don't like to go home because our Maut bosses us," Sarah blurted out. It was the first time she had spoken, and now she wished she hadn't.

"Oh, yes, Sadie Zook is helping out at your place, isn't she?" Regina asked.

"Yes," Henry confirmed, "but Sarah didn't really mean what she said."

However, Sarah did mean it, only she wouldn't say it again.

"Isn't your mother getting any better?" Regina asked.

"She doesn't cough as much anymore," Henry told her.

"What's wrong? Does the doctor know?"

"I think it's something called TB," Joe informed them.

"*Was is selli* (what's that)?" Regina asked.

"Something that makes her cough a lot, and she has to stay in bed," Henry told them. "We all had to be tested to see if we have the germ."

"How did they do that?"

"They took pictures called X rays."

"Oh!" exclaimed Raymond. "I thought we Amish aren't supposed to take pictures. Does the bishop know?"

Regina laughed. "Don't you know what X rays are, Raymond? That's a picture of your inside, not the outside for pride. The one isn't *notwendich* (necessary); the other is."

Sarah decided right then that Regina was not only pretty but also smart. She skipped along beside her and tried to mimic everything Regina did. Regina removed her bonnet, so Sarah removed her bonnet. Regina began swinging her lunch pail, so Sarah swung hers. Regina stopped to tie her shoes. Sarah bent to tie her shoe, but first she had to untie it. The older girl noticed Sarah's antics and was amused and pleased.

"*Do, klein Bussli* (here, little kitten)," Regina volunteered, "*do, loss mich dei Schuh binne* (here, let me tie your shoe)."

Sarah gladly accepted. She felt so important! So she went skipping happily, humming a little tune as she entered the kitchen. There she encountered Sadie, who looked at her with disapproval.

"*Schtobb sell grummle* (stop that muttering)!" the Maut commanded. "What were you grumbling about?"

"I wasn't grumbling," Sarah answered. "I was singing '*Jesus liebt die kleine Kinder* (Jesus loves the little children).' But I didn't want to sing too loud because of Mom. I don't want to make too much noise."

"Humph!" snorted Sadie. "Get your clothes changed and hop to the chores. Your sister Edna has been so contrary all day, and Lisabet cried most of the time. I'll take no nonsense from you tonight, so you'd better walk straight. Oh, and your mother wants to see you as soon as you change. I hope she isn't going to *verbuppl* (baby) you. *Nau, mach schnell* (now hurry up)!"

Sarah fairly flew upstairs. She quickly slipped out of her school dress and hung it on its peg on the wall. She now wore the same dress she wore so far every night that week. The Maut had decided that it made too much washing to wear a different one each day.

"Sadie said you wanted to talk with me, Mom," Sarah began as she walked into her mother's bedroom.

"Yes, come here." She held out a frail hand to her daughter.

"Mom, you were crying. *Was ist letz* (what's the matter)?" Sarah asked in dismay.

"*Druwwel dich net* (don't trouble yourself). I'm just tired and sorry I can't take care of my family. But we must believe God will take care of us all.

"Sadie hasn't been *geduldich* (patient)

23

with Edna and Lizabet today. Help all you can, Sarah," her mom said, "and don't do anything to upset her. After supper Dad will bring you children in for *Owedgebet* (evening prayer). Maybe we can talk then."

Sarah tried her best all evening to please Sadie and things went fairly well until. . . .

Sadie was not the best cook and this evening she presented the family with meat that was not tender, potatoes only half-baked and lumpy gravy. When the children didn't eat, Father was too polite to mention anything.

Sadie asked, "Why aren't you children eating?"

Sarah made the mistake of saying, "It's not like Mom's."

Sadie didn't reply, but her look spoke volumes, and somehow Sarah knew she was in trouble.

3
Just for Sarah

When supper was ended and Sam, Sarah's father, was out of earshot, Sadie lit into Sarah.

"Why, you *Grossmaul* (big mouth)! Don't you ever say anything about my cooking again. Maybe you think you can do it better?"

Sarah began to cry.

"*Schtobb sell gebrill* (stop that crying) or I'll give you something to cry about." Sadie gave her a shove toward the sink full of dirty dishes. "Get busy and wash those pots and pans, and don't go running to your mother. She has enough trouble without your complaints."

Sarah tried hard to suppress her tears. It felt as if she was choking. She hadn't meant any harm. Sadie had asked a question, and she had given an honest answer. What had she done wrong this time? It seemed to Sarah as though she could never please the *Maut* (hired girl). Every once in a while, a few tears escaped Sarah and mingled with the sudsy dishwater.

"*Nach eins* (another thing)," Sadie scolded. "Quit using so much soap to do the dishes. It's not necessary. 'Waste not, want not,' I say. It takes a lot of work to make lye soap. By the time we save enough lard and buy the lye and borax, it doesn't come cheap."

Sarah was only half-listening to the Maut's prattle. Her mind was thinking how it was before Mother was sick and Sadie came. However, Sarah did remove the bar of soap from the dishpan of water. Homemade lye soap made things clean and their white clothes nice and white, but it was rough on one's hands. Sarah's tender skin was often next thing to bleeding. Now once more it felt as if her heart was bleeding, too.

After the dishes were put back in place, Sarah took baby Lisabet and got her ready for bed. "*Fer was brillt sie immer* (why does she always cry)?" Sarah asked her mother.

"I think she's cutting teeth," Mandy told her.

"Does that hurt the *Buppeli* (baby)?" Sarah wondered.

26

"It must at least make her very uncomfortable."

"Well, then why don't we just get them pulled like Dad did his when he had toothache the other week?" suggested Sarah.

Mother laughed. She wanted to tell her daughter that you don't pull baby teeth which are just coming in, but she began to cough.

Sadie heard Mandy coughing hard and went to give her some medicine. She ushered Sarah out of the bedroom in a hurry. After easing Mrs. Troyer's spell of coughing, she faced Sarah.

"Haven't I told you not to go in the bedroom and bother your mother? What were you doing in there?"

Sarah just looked down at the floor.

"Answer me!" demanded the Maut. "Unless your mom calls you or your dad tells you to come in, you stay out of that room. I'm asking you again: What were you doing in there?"

"I wanted to know why Lisabet cries so. You told me to feed her bottle of milk to her, but she wouldn't take it. She just cries and cries."

"Your mom can hear that she cries a lot. You need not tell her. What did you expect her to do about it? Lisabet is cutting teeth, and that makes her *gridlich* (fussy)," Sadie explained.

"Then why don't they pull the teeth like they did my dad's?" Sarah asked.

"*Ich hab geglaabt du weescht besser* (I would have thought you would know better)," Sadie said disgustedly. "You don't pull babies' teeth. They need those once they learn to eat." In spite of herself, Sadie actually laughed.

After Sam Troyer came back from checking all barn doors and other out-buildings, he called his family to the bedroom for evening devotions. The hired girl was also invited — indeed expected — to join the rest. Mother's TB had passed the contagious stage, so the children gathered around her bed for this special time of fellowship.

In his deep voice, Sam read a portion of Scripture. Then as they all knelt, he prayed from the prayer book, always ending with *Unser Vater* (Our Father), the Lord's Prayer. Sarah understood little of the reading and prayer, but when she asked, her parents patiently explained.

Once Sarah had asked the meaning of "*Und vergib uns unfere Schulden, wie wir unsern Schuldigern vergeben.*" Father told her that we are asking God to forgive us our sins as we forgive others.

"If someone does something to you that isn't nice, you must forgive that person if you want God to forgive you when you do wrong. Do you understand?" Samuel Troyer asked.

Sarah thought she did. Then that meant she could not stay angry when Sadie Zook was unkind. She would try to forgive, but for her it wouldn't be easy.

Mandy Troyer improved enough within the next few weeks so she was able to eat her meals at the table with her family. Part of each day she spent in her rocker in the living room.

"Sadie," she said one day, "I'd like for you to fetch my oldest dresses. I'll show you which ones are worn in spots. Those you can cut up to make a few new dresses for Sarah. I didn't realize how tall she's getting. We'll hand her dresses on down to Edna. You do know how to run the sewing machine, I'm sure."

"Of course I do," Sadie answered quietly.

"I'll do the hand sewing," Mrs. Troyer volunteered. "That should help some."

By a week later, Sadie had cut out enough material for three dresses for Sarah. One would be brown, and the other two dark blue. Sarah would have chosen lavender since her best friend, Katie, had a lavender dress, and Sarah loved it. Regina also had a lavender one.

However, the Maut declared, "Lavender shows the dirt more. Anyway, it's just for you, Sarah, so dark colors are good enough."

Sadie hurried with the dressmaking. It was not her favorite thing. As a result, the dresses were ill-fitting, even though she used a standard Amish pattern. To Sarah and her mother, the garments looked sloppy.

"I don't like them," Sarah told her mom.

"Shh! Sadie may hear you. Perhaps she did the best she could. Once I can do my own work, I'll fix them to fit better."

That gave Sarah hope.

The next Sunday after church, Sarah heard the Maut talking to another hired girl. As was often the case, they were sharing the week's happenings.

"I made a couple of dresses for Mandy Troyer's oldest girl," Sadie reported. "I don't believe Mandy or her daughter think they fit right. But it's just for Sarah, so to my notion, it's good enough."

Sarah's self-worth took a downward plunge. *Am I nobody? Doesn't God love me?*

4

The Best Sunday Ever

It was a between Sunday. That meant no church services for the South District. The *Maut* (hired girl) had gone home on Saturday evening after supper. She needed some time off. Before leaving, Sadie prepared things easy to cook or warm up to tide the Troyer family over until her return on Monday morning.

Whenever South District had services, the Maut stayed so Samuel and the children could go to church. Mr. Troyer helped with household duties while the Maut was gone. Rain was coming down heavily, washing the earth clean.

"*Reggedrobbe, Reggedrobbe, wann duhst du schtobbe* (rain drop, rain drop, when will you stop)?" Sarah chanted, gazing out the window.

"Looks more like it's raining cats and dogs to me," Henry remarked.

"How could it rain cats and dogs?" Edna asked.

"That's just a saying people use when they mean it's raining real hard," Father said. "*Unneedich Wadde* (unnecessary words)."

"Anyway," Sarah added with a laugh, "picture that!"

"Picture what?" Edna wanted to know.

"Why, how would it look if it could rain cats and dogs?"

They both giggled.

"All right," directed Father, "get these dishes done up, and after I read from the Bible, you may play in the hayloft. I fixed that rope swing so it's safe. Mom isn't feeling as well again, so maybe it would be better if the house is quiet for a while."

Although they were sorry Mother was not well, the children were eager to play in the loft. The sound of rain on the barn roof was pleasant. Sarah thought the task of washing dishes was a never-ending one, but this time she went at it with gusto.

The boys started for the barn right after the Bible reading, dashing through the rain and stomping in as many puddles as they could. It felt good and cool to their bare feet.

"I wish the boys would wait for us," Edna complained.

"Just hurry and tie your scarf; we won't lose much time," Sarah promised her. "We have all afternoon to play."

Sarah and Edna splashed in the rain puddles, too. It made them giggle as the water sometimes *spritzed* (sprayed) their faces.

"Come on up, girls," Joe called as he heard his sisters in the feedway down below. "Watch how high I can swing." He gave himself a mighty push and went from one side of the barn to the other.

"Let me have a turn," Henry begged.

"I can't stop," Joe told them.

"*Ach* (oh), Joe, you can too!" Sarah exclaimed.

"No, really, I can't. I'm going too fast."

"Well, then, we'll help you stop," declared Henry.

As Joe came swinging by, Sarah and Henry both grabbed for the rope. The sudden jerk slowed Joe, but it knocked Sarah and Henry off their feet. They tumbled into the loose hay. How they laughed at this sudden turn of events!

"*Wie viel Meile per Schtund warst du umgeh* (how many miles per hour were you going)?" Henry jokingly asked Joe.

"I don't know," his brother answered, "but I think it was over the speed limit!"

What fun my brothers are, thought Sarah. Some children would be angry when things like this happened, but not Joe and Henry. Sure, they scrapped sometimes, as all children do, but not often.

Each had a turn on the rope swing. Then Joe had an idea.

"Say, I believe two of us can swing at the same time," he told his siblings.

"Really?" Sarah wasn't so sure. "How can we do that?"

"*Yah* (yes)," Henry added, "there's only one loop for our foot."

"You stand facing me and put your foot on top of mine," Joe said.

"Ach, I'd be too heavy."

"No," Joe insisted. "Let's try."

"Okay. Here I come!" shouted Henry. They started out, but right away his foot slipped off Joe's. It was a good thing, because they found the loop was wide enough for two to stand in. After a while, they tired of swinging and made little tunnels in the hay.

"I hear something," Edna squealed as she emerged from one of the tunnels. "Sarah, I'm scared. *Was is es* (what is it)?" she asked, clinging to her sister.

"I don't hear anything," Sarah assured her.

"*Well, ich hab* (well, I did)," Edna insisted. "Maybe it's a bear."

"*Ach, wie kindisch* (oh, how childish)!" Henry laughed. "How would a bear get up our hayloft ladder?"

"I don't know," Edna replied, "but I know I heard something."

"All right," Sarah told the boys. "Go in that tunnel, and see if you hear any noises."

Joe and Henry lost no time diving into the opening. Soon Sarah and Edna heard their shouts.

"We found it! We found it!" they yelled.

Edna was really frightened now. "Maybe we'd better go back to the house," she suggested, still holding onto her sister's apron.

"No," Sarah answered. "If it was something bad, the boys would have told us to run. They sound excited to me."

Indeed they were excited and so were the girls when the boys came from the tunnel holding two baby kittens.

"*Busslin* (kittens)!" Joe exclaimed, holding a black-and-white ball of fluff for them to look at. Henry was holding a tiny black one.

"There are two more in a hole by the side of the tunnel with their mama," he added.

35

"Oh, aren't they *schnuck* (cute)?" Edna reached out. "Let me hold one."

"Just a little," Joe told her. "The mother will move them if we play with her babies too long."

Sarah held the black-and-white one, and Edna took the other kitten.

"We'll put them back," Sarah offered.

"Be careful," Joe warned. "Hissy arched her back and spit at us when we took her *Busslin*. I don't think she likes to be disturbed."

Bussli — that's what Regina called Sarah. Now she remembered that she was going to ask her parents if they would call her Sarah Regina. When they got back to the house, Mother was sitting in her rocker. Baby Lisabet was playing on a blanket on the floor. The children were glad to see that Mother was able to be out of bed.

"Now," directed Father, after hearing the news of the surprise kittens, "do your chores. After supper, if Mother feels well enough, we'll sing."

"Mom and Dad," Sarah ventured to ask, "would you make my name Sarah Regina?"

"*Ver was* (why)?" Father asked.

"Oh, I just like the name."

"Go, do the chores at once. If everything

goes well, I might play some guessing games with you after singing," Mother suggested.

As the children came in after having done their work, Sarah declared, "This is the best Sunday. New kittens, no Maut, and maybe I'll be Sarah Regina. Dad didn't say no. Yes, it's the best Sunday ever!"

5

What's in a Name?

Mother felt better than she had for some time. She was coming to the table for meals again. Sometimes she asked the *Maut* (hired girl) if there was hand-sewing or mending to be done. One evening after supper, she sat mending the children's stockings.

"Sarah, are you girls finished with the dishes?" she asked her oldest daughter.

"*Yah* (yes), Mom, we are," Sarah answered.

"Come, then, and sit here by me. I want to teach you how to mend stockings."

Obediently, Sarah pulled up a chair alongside her mother.

"Now," instructed Mother, "watch carefully. First you turn the stocking inside out. Next pull it over this wooden egg."

"*En holzich Oi* (a wooden egg)!" exclaimed Sarah. "That's no egg!"

"I know that," Mother told her. "*Guck*

mol (look once). Isn't it shaped like an egg? It's made of smooth wood, so we call it the *holzich Oi*."

"Anyway, as long as I don't have to eat it, I don't care what its name is."

That caused Sarah to remember that she wanted to be called Sarah Regina. Maybe she would ask Mother once more. For now, though, she must learn to mend.

"Is this right?" Sarah asked, holding up the stocking pulled over the wooden piece for her mother to inspect.

"*Yah, das is gut* (yes, that's good). Next we place the patch over the hole and secure it with pins, like this." Mandy did it for her the first time. "I'll start the sewing for you. You must be careful of the pins. As you sew past each pin, remove it. Take nice, even stitches, like this."

It looked so easy as Mother's needle stitched back and forth. When Sarah tried, her stitches were long and crooked. Worse yet, she pricked her finger on one of those sharp pins.

"*Ach, Mamm, ich kann net* (oh, Mom, I can't)," Sarah wailed.

"Don't worry about it. You'll learn," Mother told Sarah. "I couldn't do it right the first few times when I was a little girl. It takes a time to avoid those pins, but you can do it. Here, let me see your finger. Why, it's almost stopped bleeding already. *Sel heelt eb die Katz en Oi legt* (that will heal before the cat lays an egg)."

Distracted by that amusing saying, Sarah smiled and went on with the task of mending once more.

Soon the boys and Edna gathered in the living room. Their work was finished for the day. Henry had some arithmetic homework, but being a good scholar, he soon completed his assignment.

"Let's play a guessing game," Sarah suggested. "We can play while we work, can't we, Mom?"

"*Ach, yah,*" her mother assured her. "My parents often played teaching games with me as I was growing up."

"Oh, tell us about it. Did you have a favorite game?" Joe asked.

"Wait a minute," Father said, looking up from the farm magazine he was reading. "We don't want Mother to overdo it, now. Just because she feels better, we can't ask too much."

"*Ach,* Samuel, I want to," his wife answered. "It isn't often that I get a chance to spend time with *die Kinner* (the children). I feel good enough."

"If you're sure, but once you begin to get

tired, then quit," Sam told her.

"*Ich verschpreche* (I promise)," Mandy answered.

The Maut brought two pails of popcorn ears and a large dishpan for the boys and Edna to work on. The popcorn was home-grown and needed shelling. It had been spread out to dry on the attic floor and now was ready.

"Don't get those kernels all over the floor," Sadie warned. "Hold them low over the dishpan so you won't make a mess." Then she turned to Mandy. "I have some letters to write, but I'll see that the little ones get to bed on time."

"You worked hard today," Mandy told her Maut. "Sam and the older ones can manage, so you don't need to help."

"*Was ewwer du saagst* (whatever you say)," Sadie replied.

"Now, Mom," Sarah coaxed after Sadie left for her room upstairs, "tell us a game you used to play."

"We'll do better than that. Let's play it just like I used to. First, I'll give you an easy one. I'll think of a Bible character, telling you something about him or her, and you must name the person I'm thinking of.

"You'll get three hints if you can't guess

41

it on the first or second try, but only three. Then I'll tell you if you still don't know. The first one to guess right will then have a turn. I'll make the first one easy. Here it is: my father loved me very much and gave me a coat of many colors. What is my name?"

"I know!" Henry exclaimed. "It's Joseph."

"*Du bist recht* (you're right)," Mother confirmed. "Now it's your turn."

"All right, here's my riddle," Henry began. "I was a little boy whose parents thought I was lost."

No one guessed it.

"Give us the second hint," the children begged.

"My parents found me in the temple."

"It must have been Jesus," Sarah guessed. She was right, so now it was her turn.

"Even though I was king, I was sad" was her first clue. Since there were many kings, some bad, some good, no one knew whom she meant. Her next sentence gave another tip: "I threw a spear at David."

Mother asked, "Could it be King Saul?"

"Yes," Sarah replied.

"Well," declared Mandy, "since I've had a turn, we'll let Edna do this one."

"I'm ready!" Edna exclaimed, jumping up and down. "We traveled far."

"That's not much of a hint," the other children complained. "Give us another."

"All right," Edna agreed. "We came from Oregon."

"I don't remember reading anything about travelers from Oregon in my Bible," Sarah commented.

"What's your last clue?" Mother asked.

"We were three kings," Edna added.

How they laughed when they realized Edna was referring to the song "We Three Kings from Orient Are." Edna was rather miffed at their laughter until Mother assured her she did well and it was an honest mistake.

"We've guessed a lot of names, and now it's bedtime," Mother told them.

"That was fun," said Sarah, "but I want to ask you and Dad if you would please give me a middle name and call me Sarah Regina."

"The name Sarah is what we gave you when you were born," Father stated. "It's a good name, and I see no reason to add another. What's in a name, anyway? It's not the name that makes the person good or bad. Rather, I'd say it's the person that makes the name.

"Go on to bed now, Sarah. Get the *Buppeli* (baby) ready for her crib. Fix her bottle. I'll help Mother get settled in."

Sarah obeyed, but all the while she wondered if she couldn't be just as good if her name was Sarah Regina instead of just plain Sarah.

As she put baby Lisabet in her crib, she vowed to name her first daughter Regina. What's in a name indeed! *Well, some names are prettier than others,* she thought. *Someday I'll have a beautiful daughter with a beautiful name.*

6

A Turn for the Worse

Things had seemed to be better at the Troyer house. Mother's coughing had been less severe, and baby Lisabet had cut her first teeth. Sarah was happier than she had been for some time.

"I did want my name to be Sarah Regina," she told her brother Henry, "but if Mom gets well again, that's all I ask."

"*Yah* (yes)," Henry answered, "that's the most important thing. Just think! We wouldn't need a *Maut* (hired girl) anymore."

"*Ach* (oh) my!" exclaimed Sarah. "Wouldn't that be wonderful! I'd be glad to do the *Arwet* (work) if only I were older. Why is it such a long time from one birthday to the next? It seems I'll be eleven forever."

"Don't say that," Henry urged. "Mom and Dad told us forever never ends. You know you will have a birthday, then you'll be twelve."

"But it takes such a long time," Sarah complained.

"What's so important about being twelve, anyway?" Henry asked his sister.

"Well, if I'd be older, maybe we could get along without Sadie."

"Mom seems to be better, and maybe before long we won't need a Maut," Henry said.

That thought encouraged Sarah once more. She went on with her task of filling the oil lamps and cleaning the lamp chimneys. Since electricity was forbidden, kerosene or gas lamps were used.

In the Troyer home, gas lamps were used in the living room and the kitchen, but smaller rooms and bedrooms upstairs and down were lit by dim oil lamps. Gas lamps shone brighter but were too dangerous for children to operate. Only grown-ups or the Maut did that.

As Sarah was carefully pouring oil into the small funnel, Sadie entered the room.

"Aren't you finished yet?" she snapped. "I saw you and Henry in here talking while you should have been working. Both of you were fiddling away time. If you wouldn't poke around so, I'd have less to do. *Mach schnell* (hurry up)." She snapped Sarah's arm with a towel she was carrying.

Sarah jumped, spilling kerosene on her dress, across the table, and onto the floor.

"You're so *doppich* (clumsy). Watch what you're doing!" Sadie scolded. "For a girl your age, you're the most *doppich* one I've ever seen. Don't you know how to do anything right? You can just wear that dress for the rest of the evening, that's what!" She marched over to the hand pump to wet the towel she had in her hand. Sarah heard her mumbling as she went.

Fighting back the tears, Sarah finished her work and returned the lamps to their proper places. Then she got rags and a bucket of hot sudsy water to clean the kerosene off the table and floor. She scrubbed them again with clear water.

Sarah wanted so much to run and change into clean clothes. Edna complained about the strong smell of the kerosene.

"What's that on your apron and dress?" she asked her sister.

Before answering, Sarah looked to see if Sadie was around. When she was sure the coast was clear, she told Edna the complete story.

"Why won't she let you change?" her sister wondered.

"I don't know, but I'm sure Mom would," Sarah told her. "But if I go into her room, Sadie will be more upset."

Sarah didn't need to go to her mother's room. Mandy had been resting most of the afternoon and now decided to sit in her rocker a while.

"*Was schmack ich* (what do I smell)?" she asked Sadie. "*Es schmackt gewiss wie Lichteel* (it certainly smells like lamp oil)." She began to cough violently from the fumes.

"Ach, my," Sadie answered, as though alarmed. "Sarah spilled kerosene while filling the lamps. She's setting the table for supper and must have forgotten to wash up and change her clothes."

"Well, I think she should change right away," Mandy gasped between spells of coughing.

"Yah, so do I." Sadie made a show of agreeing with Mandy as she made her way to the kitchen.

"Now see what you've done!" Sadie accused Sarah. "That kerosene smell made your Mother cough so hard again. Go, clean up, and change into something else so we can stand being near you. Hurry up and get back here to help put supper on."

This was all said in tones that Mandy couldn't hear. Sarah left the table-setting and hurried to the wash basin. She wondered what changed the Maut's mind, but didn't stop to question her.

At the supper table, Father and the boys asked about the kerosene smell. It was hard to get rid of. Even though Sarah had scrubbed and scrubbed, it still lingered.

The next morning Mandy Troyer was not feeling as well. She had coughed a good part of the night, and that left her weak and exhausted.

"I think I'd better take you to see Dr. Humes," Father told her. "As soon as the boys and I get the oats and corn sacked and loaded for grinding, I'll be in to get ready."

Mandy didn't want to go. She was so tired, and yet she didn't know what else to do. How she wanted to be well again and able to take care of her family! Sarah was glad it was a school day so she wouldn't be alone with the Maut.

Sadie helped Mrs. Troyer get dressed for the visit to her doctor. She combed her hair and put it up in the traditional hair style of an Amish woman: parted in the center, combed straight back, and pinned in a bun at the nape of her neck. She tied a white covering on her head and laid out her shawl and bonnet. How thin and frail Mandy was! Not at all like the hired girl, who was robust and hefty.

You would think, Sadie mused to herself, *she could at least comb her own hair and put on her covering, bonnet, and shawl.*

"I don't know if I can stand the trip to town," Mandy murmured. Sarah wished her mother needn't go. Perhaps, though, the doctor would find some way to make her well this time. With that thought in mind, Sarah started out with her brothers for school. She soon joined her friend Regina.

"Well, hello, *Bussli* (kitten)," Regina greeted her. "What have you been doing?"

Sarah told her about spilling the kerosene, the Maut's sharp words, and her mother's coughing spells.

Regina's heart went out to her. "Want to share a book with me for morning singing?" she asked.

That would be wonderful, but bigger girls always sat together. "Do you really want me to?" Sarah asked hopefully.

"I really do," her friend answered. The day looked brighter now.

That evening Father couldn't hide his

concern, and the children knew something was wrong. The house seemed so quiet. Even Edna had quit her usual chatter.

"*Was ist letz, Dat* (what's wrong, Dad)?" Sarah asked.

"It's Mom. She's taken a turn for the worse. The doctor thinks I should take her to a warmer, drier climate. All the while I thought she was getting better, and now this." Sam choked up as he spoke.

Sarah didn't know where a warmer, drier climate was, but she wished her mother hadn't taken a turn for the worse.

7

A Trick to Every Trade

Grandma and Grandpa Troyer came to see how their daughter-in-law was doing.

"*Es sie nix besser* (isn't she any better)?" Grandma Clara asked.

"I'm afraid not," her son told her. "The doctor recommends that I take her to a different climate. He thinks that may help."

"But where?" *Mammi* (Grandma) asked. "Where does he say to go?"

"*Ach,* he mentioned Arizona," Samuel answered his mother.

"But that's so far away. Could you find a house right away? What about *die Kinner* (the children)? Do you plan on taking them along? And your farm! Who would do the farming?"

"Don't think I haven't thought about all these things, Mom. Mandy and I haven't made up our minds yet for sure."

Grandpa Leroy had been trying to listen

to the conversation with one ear while the children vied for his attention. Finally, after satisfying them with peppermint candies, he promised, *"Mir tun was mir kenne* (we'll do what we can)."

"Do you think your *Maut* (hired girl) will stay on if you can't take the family?" Grandma asked.

"I don't know. I haven't asked her yet because we aren't sure if we're going," Samuel stated.

"Ach, Mammi, you ask too many questions," *Dawdy* (Grandpa) objected.

Sarah heard Grandma ask whether Sadie would stay if her parents decided to go. It struck a nameless dread in her heart. She confided in her brothers late in the day.

"Was tun mir (what will we do)?" she asked. "Sadie is mean enough when Mom and Dad are here. What will she be like when they are gone? Oh, I hope they don't leave us here with her. I hope they don't go!" she half sobbed.

"But, Sarah," Henry asked, "if it makes Mom well, don't you want her to go to Arizona?"

"Well, of course, I want Mom to feel good again, but I don't want to stay here with Sadie."

"We can't always have what we want,"

Joe commented. He had heard Sarah and Henry talking as he entered the milk house.

"It seems that we can't have anything we want when Sadie is around," Sarah complained.

"Shh!" Henry warned. "Here she comes. Get busy."

"What are you children *schtooffling* (poking around) in here for?" the Maut asked. "Does it take the three of you to get the milk pails and cart out to the barn?" She gave Sarah a push toward the door. "You haven't gathered the eggs yet. Just because *Dawdies* (the grandparents) are here, don't think you can do as you please. Now get to the chores."

Sarah wanted to ask if *Dawdies* (the grandparents) were staying for supper, but she refrained. Gathering eggs was not her favorite task. Some of the hens were sassy and refused to leave their nests. When Sarah reached under them for the eggs, the fowls sometimes pecked her hand.

Dawdies were still there when she took the basket of eggs to the house. Her father and Dawdy were coming out as Sarah stepped inside.

"Why, Sarahlie!" Grandpa exclaimed, using his pet name for Sarah. "Sarahlie, *du warst um heile* (you've been crying)! *Was is do letz* (what's wrong here)?"

Sarah was embarrassed that Dawdy could tell she'd been crying. She didn't answer right away.

"*Saag um Dawdy* (tell Grandpa)," Leroy Troyer urged.

He took his big red handkerchief from the pocket of his coat and bent down to dry her tears. "Blow your nose." She blew hard. "Tell me now," coaxed Grandpa.

Her father, waiting patiently, also encouraged his daughter: "Sarah, what happened?"

Sarah took a deep breath. "*Die Hinkel beisse mich* (the hens bite me), the Maut yells at me, and now our mom and dad will go away." In spite of herself, Sarah began to cry again.

"Sarah," her dad comforted her, "it isn't sure that Mom and I will go, and if you listen to the Maut, I don't know why she would yell at you. I've never heard her do that. I'd better get out to the barn and help the boys. Later we'll talk about Mom and what is best. Put those eggs down in the basement now and help Sadie with supper. Dawdies are staying."

"You go on and tend to things in the barn," Dawdy told Samuel. "I want to show Sarahlie how to get hens off the nest so they won't *beisse* (bite) her," he chuckled. "Chickens and hens don't bite you; they peck."

They went back to the hen house. "Watch carefully," instructed Grandpa Leroy. "The secret is, you must be quick."

Almost faster than the eye could follow, Dawdy covered the hen's head with his hand, gently pinning it down. The chicken's feathers were ruffled, but she was helpless. Dawdy reached his other hand underneath her warm body and easily removed the eggs Sarah had left. It looked so easy.

"Now you try it," Grandpa urged.

The minute Sarah's hand appeared above the hen, a warning squawk sounded and the chicken's head shot out toward her. Sarah instinctively jerked back her outstretched hand. "She doesn't like me," Sarah lamented.

"When she brings her head up towards you, be quick. Here, I'll show you again."

Over and over they went through the game until Sarah could do it. "Look, Dawdy, now I can do it!" Sarah exclaimed. "She didn't even bite me. Let me try again." Sarah performed this feat half a dozen times, exclaiming, *"Ich hab's geduh* (I did it)!"

"Yes, you did, Sarahlie. And now we'd better let these old biddies rest for the night. I want to see if I can be of any help to your dad or the boys. I believe your dad said you should help the Maut with supper."

Sarah skipped happily to the house. She had such a kind Dawdy. For the first time in her life, Sarah wished it were time to gather eggs. Her happiness was short-lived. As she appeared in the kitchen after washing up, Sadie glared at her.

"Where have you been?" the Maut demanded.

"Dawdy was showing me a good way to gather eggs," Sarah replied.

"There's only one way to do that," the Maut spat out in disgust.

"No, Dawdy showed me a trick. He said, 'There's a trick to every trade.' "

"A trick to get out of work, I suppose. Set the table and don't —"

Sadie didn't finish her scolding, for just then Mammi Clara walked in with baby Lisabet. "Sarah sure is a *grossie Hilf* (big help)," she remarked to Sadie as she watched Sarah set the table.

The Maut grunted her response.

"Oh, Mammi," Sarah exclaimed. "I learned a trick tonight. Dawdy showed me how to gather eggs so the hens can't bite me — I mean, peck."

"Yah, I know how you do that. Long ago your Dawdy taught me that same trick. It always worked for me," Mammi declared. Sarah knew it would work for her, too.

8

God Sees the Sparrow

The wind had been blowing vigorously all day. It seemed to pick up in strength as the children made their way home from school once more. Sarah turned around, trying to walk with her back toward it to shelter her face. Soon she found that was difficult. She stumbled and fell behind the other walkers.

"Hey, *Bussli* (kitten)," called Regina. "What are you doing? Come on! The wind may carry you *fatt* (away)."

Sarah only understood part of what Regina said. She heard Regina call her, but the strong gusts of wind seemed to carry the words away into the air. However, she turned and, pushing her small form against the gale, made her way to her friend's side.

Regina had kindly waited for her. Then both girls walked side by side, bending into the wind. Neither spoke much since it was not easy to hear each other.

Sarah was glad when she reached home. She tried to thank Regina, but her friend only waved and went on. *I wish Regina were home, too,* Sarah thought. *Well, she doesn't have far to go.* Even though Sarah was cold on the outside, she felt warm inside because she really liked her friend.

The boys had gone on ahead of their sister and were already preparing for the outside work. As soon as Sarah struggled through the door, Sadie started scolding.

"Where have you been?" she demanded. "Your brothers have been home for quite a while."

"It was hard to walk in the wind," Sarah explained.

"The boys got home on time. Why couldn't you?"

Sarah didn't dare remind the *Maut* (hired girl) that the boys were stronger.

"Well, *mach schnell* (hurry up) and change your clothes. *Es is Arwet zu duh* (there is work to do)."

Sarah quickly obeyed. Outside work would be difficult in this strong wind, but chores won't wait.

The cows and horses stood in huddles by the barnyard, eager to be taken into the shelter of the loafing shed or the barn. As Sam opened the gate, there was a pushing and stomping of the anxious animals to get inside. Mr. Troyer almost got trampled. He was thankful that he opened the gate tonight instead of asking one of his sons to do it.

"We'll leave the livestock inside tonight. It isn't fit to have them out in this weather."

Sarah set out to do her part of the evening chores. As she struggled to push open the door of the hen house, a huge gust of wind slammed it shut on her arm. It hurt badly. Again she tried to open the door, and again it closed with a bang. The third time she succeeded in getting inside the hen house.

Her arm was paining her badly, but she gathered eggs as well as she could. Making her way back to the house was another struggle. The wind nearly whipped the basket of eggs out of her hands.

"What took you so long this time?" Sadie asked crossly.

"I couldn't open the door, and when I finally did, it blew shut and caught my arm. It hurts so bad." Tears appeared in Sarah's eyes.

"*Ach* (oh), you act as if it's broken. You'd better get to the barn before they come looking for you."

Just then Henry opened the kitchen door, letting in several gusts of wind.

"See," Sadie scolded Sarah, "I told you they'd come looking for you. Now get!"

"No," Henry countered her, "Sarah doesn't have to help with the milking. Dad said it's too stormy out for her. We men can do the chores tonight."

Sarah was grateful. No way could she have milked cows tonight, not with the pain she felt. Mother was resting on her chair, and Sarah heard her call.

Sadie had gone to the basement for some canned peaches, so Sarah answered her mother's call. "*Was wit* (what do you want), Mom?"

"Oh, Sarah, I'm so glad to see you're all safely home from school. That wind sounds so fierce. Could you bring me a drink of water?"

"*Yah* (yes), Mom, I will."

Sarah made her way to the water pail in the kitchen and dipped a glassful, careful not to spill any. Since she couldn't bend her left arm, it wasn't easy. She had to set the glass in the sink and try to fill it that way.

"Why, Sarah!" exclaimed Mother. "Why do you hold your left arm so funny? You were crying, too. *Was is letz* (what's wrong)?"

"Ach, Mom, when I went to gather the eggs, I couldn't keep the wind from blowing the door shut. I pinched my arm, and it hurts *wunderbaar* (terribly)."

"*Kumm mol do* (come here once) and let me look at it. Ach my! I'm afraid it's broken. It's swollen so I can't even pull your sleeve up. Go tell Sadie to come in here right away."

"Look," Mandy told her Maut, "I believe Sarah's arm is *gewiss verbroche* (really broken). See how it's swelled up. Bring the scissors to cut her dress sleeve."

Mother was ready to snip the seam of Sarah's sleeve, but she began to cough violently. Handing the scissors to Sadie, she indicated with a wave of her hand for the Maut to perform the task.

Sadie slowly and even gently cut away at the fabric. Sarah was glad her mother was present, or else the Maut might not have been so kind.

"The arm is turning a bluish color," Mandy observed, once her coughing had subsided.

"It doesn't look good," Sadie remarked, "but I'm sure it can be fixed." Then she told Sarah, "Don't worry about helping with supper. Edna can set the table. You just rest and play with Lisabet if you want to."

Sarah appreciated Sadie speaking kindly to her since it happened so rarely.

When the men blew in from the outside, Mandy called her husband to her side at once. "Are you feeling that much worse?" Sam anxiously asked.

"It's not me, it's Sarah," she told Sam. "Look at her arm. I'm afraid it's broken."

One look confirmed that fact. "*Yah, du bist recht* (yes, you're right). It's a bad break, too. The doctor will need to set it, but there is no way we can take her in this storm. The top [high-topped] buggy would blow over. The nearest phone is at Yancy's, but I can't send any of the boys the two miles to call. It's beginning to thunder and lightning.

"All I know to do is give her pain pills and apply some ice. We'll chip some from the block in the icebox and put it in a bag. She can lay the ice on her arm to keep the swelling down. First thing in the morning, we'll take a trip to town, Sarah."

There was little sleep for anyone in the Troyer home that night. Mother coughed a lot. Sarah whimpered from pain. Father and the boys worried about Sarah and Mother.

The Maut's sleep was interrupted as she took care of the family's needs. Only baby

Lisabet slept. She was young enough yet that she didn't have a care in the world.

"Oh, if only I were able to take care of my family," Mandy moaned. "I feel so helpless."

"*Druwwel dich net* (don't trouble yourself)," her husband comforted her. "Everything will work out all right. The Lord knows our needs. We've called upon him, and if his eye is on the sparrow, I know he watches over us."

"*Du bist recht* (you're right)," Mandy answered. "I know his eye is on the sparrow, and upon our house as well."

9

I Hurt Too

Morning couldn't come soon enough for Sarah. The swelling in her arm had subsided considerably, but the pain remained.

"Doc Humes won't be in his office before nine," Father remarked, "so I can help the boys do the morning work. We should still get there in time to be his first patient."

Sarah sincerely hoped so. Had she known what lay in store for her, she would not have been so willing.

"*Was fer Rock soll ich waere* (what dress shall I wear)?" Sarah asked.

"You'd better wear the same one you were wearing when this happened," Mother said.

"But Mom, that's my chore dress. Besides, the one sleeve is cut. What will the doctor think? I don't want him to think I'm *kutslich* (sloppy)!" Sarah fretted.

"Chances are he's seen worse. Slip a clean *aiermellos Schatz* (sleeveless apron) over your dress. It'll hide any stains. Go now, and let Sadie help you. I'm so tired." Mrs. Troyer began to cough, and Sarah wished she wouldn't have bothered her.

"Mom said to get you to help me with my dress and apron," Sarah told the *Maut* (hired girl).

"Are you completely helpless?" Sadie asked. "What are you wearing?"

"Mom told me to wear the dress I had on when I broke my arm."

"That old *Huddel* (rag)!" Sadie remarked. "Well, I suppose some people don't care how they look. Come on, then. I suppose we would need to cut the sleeve of another dress to get your arm into it. No use ruining two dresses. Here, put your hand through this arm hole," Sadie ordered.

Sarah tried to oblige. "I can't lift my arm."

"*Ach* (oh), don't be so *kindisch* (childish)," Sadie exclaimed, taking the broken arm and raising it swiftly. Sarah's eyes filled with tears, and she tried to suppress a scream. Fearing that Mrs. Troyer might hear her daughter's outcry, the Maut became more gentle. She buttoned Sarah's dress down the back and slipped a clean, blue apron over it. Sarah knew that when she began to wear women's garb, such as capes and belt aprons, she would not be allowed to have any buttons.

"*Bist du faddich* (are you ready)?" Samuel Troyer asked his daughter.

"*Yah, Dat, ich bin* (yes, Dad, I am)," replied Sarah.

"Well, then, let's go. If we get there first, maybe I can do a little grocery shopping and still get home in time to fix that gate old Nebb broke through." Old Nebb was Sam's prize bull. Nebb had helped build up a good dairy, but he was hard to handle.

The horse started out at a good pace as soon as Sam and Sarah turned onto the roadway.

"Now," Sam began, "Sarah, I want to prepare you for something."

"*Was is es, Dat* (what is it, Dad)?" she asked.

"When Dr. Humes sets your arm, it will hurt, but only for a short while. Sometimes in order to make things better, we have to go through some pain. Just try to stand it as well as you can. I wish I could take the pain for you."

"Dad, I'm scared."

Seeing the fear in his child's eyes, Sam

told her the good doctor would probably give her something to lessen the pain.

"*Bleibst du mit mir, Dat* (will you stay with me, Dad)?" Sarah asked.

"*Yah, wohl* (yes, certainly)," her father assured her.

The doctor was just unlocking his office door as Sam and his daughter came up the walk. A rather large tree limb lay across their path, blocking the way. Dr. Humes stepped outside to remove it. Sam immediately bent to help lift the branch.

"Well, Sam, some storm we had last night, but I expect you farmers could use the rain."

"That's true," Sam agreed. The two men dragged the limb aside and went into the office.

"What brings you in so early?" the doctor asked. "Is your wife worse again?"

"She seems to be, but I brought Sarah in." Everyone in the Amish settlement and the surrounding community knew each other by name.

"Oh, so it's you, Sarah. What can I do for you? Did you eat too many half-moon pies and get a tummyache?" he teased.

Sarah didn't reply. She tried to hide behind her dad. So her father answered for her. "I'm afraid she broke her arm."

"Come here, and let me take a look," Dr. Humes invited.

Trembling with fright, Sarah reluctantly obeyed. It didn't take long for the doctor to make his diagnosis. "You're right, Sam. It's a break all right. She did it up good. How did it happen?"

"She was going to gather the eggs in the storm. The wind blew the hen house door shut, catching her arm."

"I'd say this tiny arm had little chance of battling last night's gale. I'll need your help, Sam. We have to set the large bone. Do you think you can assist?"

Sam knew the doctor wondered if he could stand it to hold onto his daughter while he set the bone. But Dr. Humes did not want to frighten Sarah any more, so that's why he carefully chose his words.

"I'll do my best." How Sam wished he could take the pain for his little girl.

It was all that Sam could do to hold Sarah as the doctor began to pull on her arm. She twisted and squirmed, sobbing and pleading. Then when she thought she could take no more, the doctor gave a sharp jerk. Sarah screamed.

"Did you hear that snap?" Dr. Humes asked Sam. "We've got 'er now. It's all over, Sarah," he told his sobbing patient.

"We'll put that wing in a cast now, and you'll be good as new."

Sam was wiping sweat from his face with his big red handkerchief. "Can't you give her something for pain?"

"I'll give you some pills to take along home. I don't like to give strong sedatives to such young children. Too many things can go wrong. That's why I couldn't give her more before I set her bone. She should feel better by evening."

"How much do I owe you?"

"Sam," answered the good doctor, "you have trouble enough. Tell you what — I have plenty of yard work at my place and here at the office. If you can spare one of your boys to come and help me, we'll call it paid."

"When do you want him?"

"Any Wednesday. That's my day out of the office."

"Done," agreed Sam as he bid the doctor a good day.

Sarah tried to put her bonnet on her head, but she couldn't accomplish it with one arm in a cast and sling. Sam helped her, and then they started for home.

"Dad," Sarah cried, "why did you hold me so tight and let the doctor hurt me? Didn't you care?"

"You don't know how much I cared. I hurt too, Sarah. I hurt for you. It had to be done or else your arm would always have been crooked. Just as I hurt with you today, so our heavenly Father hurts with us as we go through hard times. But through that pain, our way will be made straight."

Sarah didn't quite understand but she laid her head against her father's shoulder, content to know he cared.

10
The Plan

Sarah loved the attention bestowed upon her because of her broken arm. Her siblings were at her beck and call. In school it was as if she were the most important student. Now that the pain was gone, it wasn't so bad. Everyone made her feel special — everyone except the *Maut* (hired girl).

"*Du meenst du bist ebbes nau* (you think you're something now)!" she told Sarah. "If I didn't know better, I'd say you broke that arm on purpose just so you'd get *verbuppled* (babied). I think you can do more with that arm in a sling than what you pretend."

Sarah wanted to tell her that Dr. Humes told her not to use it at all. She knew better and kept the hurt to herself. *Can't Sadie ever say anything kind to me?* she wondered. Well, she would just try to stay out of Sadie Zook's way as much as possible.

Edna had to take on Sarah's tasks of gathering eggs, filling kerosene lamps, sweeping the kitchen floor after each meal, and various other chores. Sarah minded baby Lisabet, set the table, and did other easy things. Six weeks after Sarah's misfortune, the doctor removed the cast.

"There, now, young miss, looks to me like your arm's good as new. And I didn't hurt you a bit this time, did I?"

Sarah shook her head, relieved that it was all over.

"Well, you stay away from hen house doors while it's storming, and you'll be all right." Doctor Humes laughed. "Say, by the way, Sam, your son did such a good job of cleaning up my place and the grounds around the office. I wonder if there's any chance I could get him to do some painting?

"My house needs some sprucing up, and the missus has been pestering me for some time to have it done. I don't seem to find the time. Besides, I'm no painter. Your Amish farm buildings always look well-kept, and I see your people doing their own work."

"Henry is no painter either; he's a farmer. But if you think he can do the job to your satisfaction, you can have him."

"Fair enough. I'd like him to start on it next week if he can."

"That would suit me fine. The sooner, the better, because I know what I must do very soon," Father answered gravely.

Dr. Humes cleared his throat and nodded. He knew what Samuel Troyer meant, and he agreed. Sarah caught the serious tone of their conversation but didn't catch the meaning. She was soon to find out.

Henry had been painting at Dr. Humes' place every Saturday for a month. He was almost finished, and the doctor was pleased.

One Sunday evening after the family's usual light supper, Sam called his family together for a talk. His somber mood frightened the children. They sensed something was amiss.

"Henry, do you suppose you can finish Doc Humes' house in two more Saturdays?" Dad began.

"Oh, sure. I can easily do it if nothing goes wrong. Why do you ask?" Henry wondered.

"It looks like I'll have to take Mom to Arizona for a while to see if the climate there will help her. You'll be needed here to help carry on while we are gone. I can get Honas Check's Alvin to help, but *you* know how I like things taken care of." There were several Alvin Schrocks in the community, and Sam was speaking of the one whose father was Check (Jake) and whose grandfather was Honas (Henry).

Henry felt good about his father's confidence in him. But Sarah wasn't pleased. She was terrified at the thought of her parents leaving. How would the Maut treat them then? "Oh, *Dat* (Dad)," she asked in a quivering voice, "how long will you and Mom be gone?"

"I don't know yet, Sarah. I hope not long."

"Can we go with you?" Edna asked.

"No, I'm afraid not," Sam answered.

"*Awwer wer gebt acht uff uns* (but who will take care of us)?" Sarah wondered. She dreaded the answer, but she had to know for sure.

"Sadie will, of course," her father told her.

That was exactly what Sarah didn't want to hear. There was only one thing to do. She would think of a plan. That's what she must do. As of right now, Sarah didn't know exactly what, but somehow she would find a way.

Time seemed to pass all too swiftly for

76

Sarah. She dreaded the day when her parents would leave. It seemed to her that the Maut was extra bossy since she knew the Troyer parents would soon be leaving.

Sarah wanted her parents to understand that Sadie was short and snappy with them. The Maut was sly enough to do this only out of earshot of Sam and Mandy, so Sarah couldn't convince them. Several times Sadie was almost caught, but she put on such an act of kindness that both of Sarah's parents felt they must have misunderstood.

Sadie was plagued with severe headaches. Sometimes she could hardly do the work required of her, but she needed the money. Her parents had both passed away, and she lived alone in the *Dawdyhaus* (wing of the main house) where her late grandparents used to live. She had to make her own way.

The years had crept up on her, and she was no longer one of the *Yunge* (young folks). She had a few spinster friends who shared with each other about their experiences of being Mauts in different homes. It wasn't always easy to be a Maut. They had many stories to tell. Some were good, some funny, and then there were the hard places to work.

Three more weeks had gone by since Sam told his family that he and Mandy must leave for a while. It was almost time to leave. He had made plans with a local man who used his van to transport Amish people on trips near or far. Honas Check's Alvin had come a week before the departure date to "learn the ropes," as Sam put it.

Alvin was a young man who had not married. He also had to make his own way. Living in a two-room shack, as he called it, he was batching it. Like Sadie, he had thought of marriage, but it seemed no one would have him. His aunt used to tell him, "There's no kettle so warped that some lid won't fit." Sadie had heard that same expression.

Mandy thought it would break her heart to leave her little family. "Sarah," she told her daughter, "you must be a brave girl while I am gone. Listen to Sadie, and try not to upset her. Help as good as you can so she doesn't have so much to do. Take good care of Lisabet. She's starting to walk now and gets into things. Be patient with her.

"I'll try to write as often as I can, and you write, too. Let me know how things are going, and be sure to read your Bible and pray that I will soon be better and can come home.

"Oh, yes, and I want you to —," but then Mandy began to cough so again she couldn't finish her sentence.

Sarah wondered what it was Mother wanted her to do. Sadie came to aid Mrs. Troyer and ushered Sarah out of the room. After Mandy's cough subsided, Sadie found Sarah in the pantry.

"You always seem to upset your mother. Stay out of her bedroom, you hear me? Wait till your folks are gone. I'll teach you right."

Sarah could have told her that Mother called her to her room, but she only thought of *the plan* she was already making. It had begun to form.

11

The Truth Revealed

Things were beginning to shape up. Father had made all the arrangements to leave by Thursday. Since this was Tuesday, Sarah reminded herself that only two days remained until her parents' departure. She longed desperately to spend much time with her Mother, but Sadie forbade that.

"You leave your mother alone," she ordered. "Your mom is weak and needs all the rest she can get. Your folks have a long trip ahead. Don't bother her with your *kindisch* (childish) questions."

"But when are they coming back?" Sarah asked. "That's all I wanted to ask her."

"*Kind* (child), how should I know? I guess when your mother gets well again. Who can tell when that will be? Not even your parents know that. Will you go and change Lisabet? She has been *gridlich* (fussy) all morning."

Sarah obeyed, but her heart felt heavy. Sadie made it sound as if it would be a long, long time before her parents returned home.

"Don't you worry, Lisabet," Sarah hushed her baby sister. "I'll take good care of you, and if I pray, God can make Mom well. Then they'll come home soon. I feel it right now. They won't be gone long. Jesus knows we need them, and Mom told me once to always pray, because he hears us."

Baby Lisabet smiled and kicked her chubby little legs. All she wanted was some attention and to feel dry and warm. Sarah loved to play with her, but she was usually called to other household tasks.

Edna also was expected to help with many indoor and outdoor tasks. This was especially evident during garden and canning season. However, since Mandy Troyer's illness kept her from the care of her baby, Sarah was more like a mother to Lisabet. Now that her little sister could crawl fast, she followed Sarah constantly.

"*Ach* (oh), Lisabet," Sarah said, "I wish I could stop and play with you, but Sadie says to get these windows done."

Sarah had been washing windows all morning. Even with the step stool, she could hardly reach the top panes. Her arms ached, but she was expected to be finished by noon. She gave a final swipe in the top corner and was ready to move to the next window.

Then it happened. Lisabet left her homemade string of empty spools and made her way to the bucket sitting by the step stool. That bright yellow bucket looked so attractive. With one hand, she reached in to splash in the water Sarah left there.

With her other hand the baby tried to balance herself, holding to the edge of the pail. It tipped over, spilling the vinegar water all over the kitchen floor. Lisabet sat down in the wet puddle and began squawking in protest.

Sarah quickly righted the empty bucket. She heard the *Maut* (hired girl) leaving her sewing and making her way to the kitchen. Sarah knew what she would hear.

"*Du doppich Meedel* (you clumsy girl)! Why don't you watch what you're doing? Anyone would know better than set that bucket where Lisabet could reach it. She's into *alles* (everything)."

Sarah could take a lot of criticism, but when Sadie talked about her baby sister making trouble, too, that was another matter. "Don't blame Lisabet," Sarah pleaded. "She's only a *Buppeli* (baby) and doesn't know what she's allowed to play with."

"For talking back to me, you'll scrub the entire kitchen floor. It's time you respect your elders."

Sadie took Lisabet and changed all her clothes. Placing her in the high chair, she tied her fast with a scarf around her middle.

"Here," she said as she gave the baby a soda cracker. "Maybe this will keep you out of mischief."

Sadie went back to the sewing machine, but not before she saw to it that Sarah was on her hands and knees scrubbing.

Mandy Troyer was almost certain she heard Sadie speaking harshly to her daughter. After the evening meal, she asked her husband if they could talk with Sarah and perhaps find out about it.

"I can't leave if the Maut is unkind to our children," she told Samuel.

That's how it happened that a meeting was called in Mandy's room. Sarah wondered what she was being called for.

"Sarah," her father began, "Mom thinks she heard Sadie scold you today. *Was hot gewwe* (what happened)?"

"I don't think Sadie wants me to tell," she answered timidly.

"Well, we want you to, so *raus mit* (out with it)."

Sarah told them everything. "Mom, I didn't mean to leave that pail for Lisabet to get into. She doesn't know better, and I didn't know where to put it."

"No, Lisabet doesn't know better," Sam agreed. "Sarah, does she *zankt* (scold) often? And does she do this to the other children?"

"Sometimes she scolds Edna, but mostly me. She doesn't say mean things to the boys, only if they track in *Dreck* (mud). Once she shook *Buppeli* Lisabet, but I shouldn't be tattling. It isn't nice to tattle, is it?" Sarah asked.

"In this case you're only answering our questions, and I don't call that tattling," Father assured his daughter.

Mandy was crying now. "Ach, Sam, we must call the other children in and talk with them."

"*Yah* (yes)," Sam agreed. "I'll get them right away."

Sarah started to leave the room, but Mother's feeble voice called to her. "Don't go, Sarah," she begged.

"But Sadie doesn't like it if I come to

your room. She says I mustn't bother you. She'll scold me again."

"Please stay," Mother insisted. "I'll tell her *I* asked you to stay."

Sarah went to her mother's bedside and took the frail hand held out to her. How thin and pale Mother looked! Father carried baby Lisabet to see Mother. He was followed by his two sons and his daughter Edna. Sadie wondered at this but went on to a few kitchen duties before retiring for the evening.

Father questioned the boys and Edna concerning Sadie's treatment of them. They confirmed what Sarah had said. Yes, at times Sadie had spoken roughly to them, but she constantly talked sharply to Sarah. Constantly!

"Why would she do that?" Father asked.

"She says I'm older than Edna or Lisabet and should know *besser* (better)."

"Well," Sam decided, "I believe the best thing to do is for us to have a talk with Sadie alone and later with all of you together."

Mother agreed, but Sarah was frightened. How would Sadie react to this?

As the children filed somberly out to the living room, Henry called Sadie. "Mom and Dad want to talk with you. Dad said to come right away."

Sadie was looking forward to a few minutes of relaxing on the porch swing and wondered what could be so important. Nevertheless, she dropped what she was doing and made her way to the bedroom.

Sam cleared his throat, unsure of how to begin. "Sit down, Sadie." He pointed to Mother's rocker. "I have to talk to you about something. It isn't easy, but I guess the best way is to be honest and begin. Mother thinks she heard you severely scolding Sarah today. Is this true, and does it happen often?"

What could she say? The truth was out, and shamefacedly, she confessed.

12

The Saddest Day

Samuel Troyer had a heart-searching talk with the hired girl and his children.

"Sadie, I know it isn't easy to take over the responsibilities of caring for other people's children. Can you try to understand that it isn't easy for the children, either? They were used to their mother, and it's a change for them."

Sadie could not face Samuel. She knew she had been too impatient many times. If only Sam and Mandy knew how many severe headaches she endured. Yet she must go on working, for this was her only source of income.

"*Ich duh besser* (I'll do better)," she promised, as tears filled her eyes.

"That's all we ask," Samuel assured her.

"It'll be so much easier for me to leave if I can believe all will be well," Mandy weakly responded.

87

"*Ich helf gut* (I'll help good)," Sarah told her parents. "Don't worry, Mom, we'll all work together like Dad said." Sarah was trying to comfort her mother, but in her heart, she wondered how they really would get along.

Dawdies (Grandparents), Mandy's parents, had promised to help out as best they could. Adam and Lucy Weaver were getting along in years. They lived in the *Dawdyhaus* (grandparents' house) on their son Reuben's farm. Uncle Reuben and his wife also offered to help. Aunt Salome, Mandy's older sister, usually came at spring housecleaning and extra busy times, so the family knew they didn't stand alone in their time of need. Yet Salome had her own family of five children to care for and another one on the way.

Father was up early on Thursday morning. He wanted to see that all was in order before leaving.

Sarah followed him to the porch. "What are you doing up so early?" Sam asked his daughter.

"I couldn't sleep, and when I heard you down here, I just wanted to talk."

"Well, what is it?"

"Will Arizona make Mom well again? Won't she cough anymore? How long do

88

you have to stay? Why can't we all live there?"

"Whoa, Sarah, *schtobb mol* (stop once). We have tried to explain all this before. *Ach* (oh), come here," Sam invited her to the swing. "*Setz dich* (seat yourself), and I will tell you again. We don't know yet if the Arizona climate will make Mother feel better and stop her cough. We hope so. All we can do is try it once and pray. I don't know how long we have to stay. Maybe a few months."

"A few months! How many?" Sarah asked.

"Well, it's August now, so in two months it would be November."

"November!" Sarah exclaimed. "That's my birthday. November the fifteenth. I'll finally be twelve then. *Ach, Dat, sel is lang* (oh, Dad, that's long)."

"It seems like a long time for you, but as you grow older, time has a way of passing quickly. Yet it can't go swiftly enough while we're apart."

"But why can't we all go and live there together like we do here?" Sarah inquired.

"If the Arizona weather is good for your mother's health, that's what we will do. But I can't take my family until I have a place for us to live. So you see, Sarah, we'll all be together soon, either in Arizona or here. Now go, get your shoes and stockings, and keep those feet dry. We don't want you getting sick." He gently patted her head as he arose from the swing and started for the barn.

Samuel had felt the longing to be alone for a few moments before the day's activities began. He needed to meditate and commune with his Maker. His daughter needed a father's understanding and assurance, which she received.

Sarah had just finished tying her shoes when Sadie came downstairs.

"Why are you up so soon?" she asked. Her voice was not harsh or scolding, and Sarah looked at her rather hesitatingly. She wasn't sure she heard right. Maybe last night's talk with her parents *had* done some good.

"Oh, I couldn't sleep anymore," Sarah answered.

"Do you think I can't take care of you while your folks are gone?" the *Maut* (hired girl) asked. Her voice had risen slightly.

"Oh, no," Sarah quickly answered, not wishing to upset the Maut. "I know you can."

"Well, then, stop fretting and get the chickens taken care of so you can get back in here and help with breakfast. We have a lot to do this morning. Your folks will leave soon, so don't poke around."

Sarah dutifully did as she was told, and in no time was helping in the house. A quietness almost like a shroud had settled over the entire place. Both sets of grandparents were coming to say their good-byes and help with last-minute packing. It was hard for the children to concentrate on their work.

Only Alvin, the hired hand, went about the chores as though he had always lived here. Sam felt he had found a dependable worker in Alvin.

"Here come Grandpa Weavers," Sarah exclaimed.

"Ssshhh," Sadie cautioned. "Don't be so noisy."

Sarah was excited but hadn't meant to be noisy.

Grandma Lucy greeted each child and then went to her ailing daughter. "*Wie fiehlst du demaiye* (how do you feel this morning), Mandy?" she asked.

"*Net so gut* (not so good)," Mandy spoke softly.

"Well, *mir hoffe* (let's hope) this trip will prove to be the answer for you," Grandma said.

"If it's God's will," her daughter responded.

"*Yah* (yes)," Lucy agreed, "if it's God's will."

Grandpa Troyers also drove in the lane and were soon surrounded by the children. As usual, Grandpa Leroy passed out wintergreen and peppermint candy and delighted in the smiles and thank-yous he received for them.

"Sarah, you didn't fill the water pail," the Maut told her. "And didn't I tell you to hang the wet dish towels out to dry on the porch line?" The porch line was a short piece of light rope stretched from one porch post to another. "Now hurry up. Mr. Mason will be here soon with his van to pick up your folks, and you won't even have your morning work done."

The Maut still spoke more quietly than usual. Somehow Sarah felt Sadie was only biding her time. Was she waiting till Sarah's parents were gone to vent her anger?

Sarah wished Sadie would quit reminding her that the taxi would be here soon. She didn't want that time to come. Perhaps Walter Mason had forgotten. Or maybe his car wouldn't start. What if he had been in an accident and couldn't — oh, she must not think of such horrible things!

Her dreams were abruptly shattered as Mr. Mason drove up just as she hung the last dish towel on the line. This was the saddest day of her life thus far. Sarah could not imagine anything sadder.

"We'll try to write as soon as we get there," Samuel Troyer told his family.

"And every day," Mandy promised in her whispering voice.

"Children, be good," Father urged.

Then they were gone, with only a dust trail following them.

13
The Plan in Action

Sarah watched the disappearing van until it became only a speck in the distance.

"Are you going to stand there all day?" Sadie asked as she came from the house with the water pail. "Bring some fresh water, and don't dawdle. Grandma Weaver wants a cool drink."

If *Dawdies* (the two sets of grandparents) hadn't been there when Samuel Troyers left, Sadie would have marched Sarah inside and put her to work right away. The other children had followed their grandparents into the house, but not Sarah. It was so hard to let go. She obediently took the water pail and filled it with the cool, clear water from the outdoor pump. As Sarah entered the kitchen, she met Grandma Troyer, who was carrying an armful of sheets and blankets.

"*Do, Mammi, loss mich* (here, Grandma,

let me)," Sarah offered as she reached for the bedding.

"Sarah, you're such a good girl and a real helper. I'm sure your mother will rest easier knowing you're such a *willich* (willing) worker."

Sarah was glad Grandma Clara felt this way, but she wished she knew her struggles. "*Ach* (oh), *Mammi*," Sarah began, "I want to be good, and I try to be good. Sometimes I don't like our *Maut* (hired girl). Then I feel bad."

"Why, Sarah!" Grandma Troyer gasped in surprise. "Why don't you like Sadie? She takes care of you, doesn't she?"

"She sees that the work gets done and cooks our meals, but, Mammi, she's bossy."

Grandma laughed. Sarah looked at her in amazement. Didn't she believe her?

"Oh, *Kind* (child), just because she tells you what to do doesn't mean she's bossy. All children need someone to oversee them. A good boss is half the work done."

She doesn't understand, Sarah thought. She wanted to tell Grandma Clara that it was the tone of voice Sadie used and her impatient attitude, but she didn't know if she should. So all Sarah said was, "*Yah* (yes), Mammi." Perhaps Sadie would be nicer since her dad had talked things over with her. Sarah truly hoped so.

Both sets of grandparents and Aunt Salome stayed for lunch and late into the afternoon. There was laundry to do, and late sweet corn and tomato juice to can. The family used lots of tomato juice in the winter. It was used to make creamy tomato gravy eaten with fried cornmeal mush.

Every Amish housewife and young girl knew how to make tomato gravy: First, bring the tomato juice to a boil. Reduce the heat and slowly stir in the sauce made of flour and rich milk or cream. Then season it with salt and pepper. Some people prefer to sweeten it a bit instead.

"Who will sleep in Mom and Dad's room?" Sarah asked Grandma Lucy as she helped put the clean sheets and blankets in place.

"I suppose the Maut will," Grandma told her.

"Well, why can't Edna and I? Oh, Mammi, I always did *winsch* (wish) I could sleep in a downstairs bedroom. It seems so far away from everything upstairs."

"*Ach, Kind,*" Grandma Lucy consoled her, "the angels watch over you just as well upstairs as they would if you slept downstairs."

"Yah, but Edna and I must go through the *dunkel* (dark) hallway, and sometimes the boys jump out and *schrecke* (scare) us."

"Since you know it's the boys, what do you need to be scared of? Anyway, Alvin will be sleeping in the boys' room, too. He'll keep them straight. Sadie needs to be downstairs to take care of baby Lisabet."

That settled that, and Sarah said no more. Both sets of grandparents went home before supper. Now the household was on its own.

"Sarah," Sadie directed the next morning, "you make the tomato gravy for breakfast, and I'll fry the mush. Be sure to mix your sauce well. If there's one thing I can't stand, it's lumpy gravy."

Sarah reached for a bowl on the second shelf of the cupboard. She wasn't quite tall enough. It slipped from the edge of the shelf and crashed into pieces on the kitchen floor.

"*Du doppich Nixnutz* (you clumsy good-for-nothing)!" Sadie scolded. "Look what you did. That was one of your mother's best serving bowls. I ought *bletsche* (to spank) you good. Maybe I just will." She took a step toward the frightened girl.

At that moment the hired hand walked into the kitchen. Sadie instantly changed, and her voice was as smooth as silk: "Sarah, no need to cry. You couldn't help it. Those cupboards are too high for you. I should have reached for the bowl myself. Here, use this bowl." She handed Sarah another one. "Don't worry. I'll clean this up." Then she looked toward Alvin. "We just had a little accident."

Sarah couldn't believe what she was hearing. Well, it wouldn't change her plan — not one bit.

The tomato gravy turned out fine, but no one seemed to be hungry. No one, that is, except Alvin and Sadie.

"You must eat, children," Sadie told the children as though she was concerned.

Sarah saw through the Maut's fickleness. *She's trying to put on a good front to impress the hired man.* Sarah knew that if Alvin weren't around, Sadie would be her usual unkind self. Well, she wouldn't stand for that.

After breakfast, the Maut went down to the truck patch. This was the chance Sarah had been waiting for. She had been told to sweep the kitchen floor and start on the basket of ironing. Instead, she rounded up Edna and told her to get baby Lisabet and the *Windelsackli* (diaper bag).

"What are you doing?" her sister asked.

"Edna, you, I, and Lisabet are going to run away."

"Run away!" Edna exclaimed. "Run away where?"

"To Regina Byler's house. It isn't far, and I know if we tell them how our Maut acts, they'll come and get our things and let us stay with them."

"Ach, do you think we should?" Edna protested. "Mom and Dad won't know where we are. How can they write to us?"

"Quit asking questions and hurry before Sadie comes and catches us. Put some diapers and the baby bottles in the *Windelsackli*."

Edna did as she was told, and soon two young girls, the largest carrying a baby, were walking down the dusty road to their neighbor's place.

"What about the boys? They won't know where we are."

"They'll find out when the Bylers bring us back to pick up our clothes," Sarah assured Edna. "The Maut isn't snappy with the boys like she is with me. I think she was going to hit me when I broke the bowl this morning.

"The boys can bring us Mom and Dad's letters. Anyway, I had this plan for a long time, so today we're going to do it. We'll come back when Mom and Dad come home. They'll understand."

Edna wasn't so sure.

14
Please Say Yes!

"*Was in der Welt kummt do* (what in the world comes here)?" Mrs. Byler exclaimed as she spotted Sarah.

"Why, it's Sarah Troyer and her sisters," Regina informed her mom.

"Why would they be coming here so early in the day? And even bringing the baby! Something must be *wunderbaar letz* (terribly wrong)."

"Well, let's find out." Regina dropped her hoe and ran to the lane. Even though garden things were fairly well finished for the summer, Dena Byler would not let the weeds take over. She wisely instructed her children:

Let weeds lie beneath the snow,
By spring you'll have much more to hoe.

Regina and her mother liked to do their

weeding early in the morning before the sun rose to its fullest. Now both hurried to greet the Troyer girls.

"What brings you here so early? Is anything wrong?" Dena asked.

"We want to know — may we stay with you till Mom and Dad come back?" Sarah asked.

"Why?" Mrs. Byler asked. "Why would you want to stay with us? Isn't your *Maut* (hired girl) helping out anymore?"

"*Yah* (yes)," Sarah answered, "but she isn't good to me and sometimes not to the baby or Edna. I don't want to go home. Can't we just stay with you?"

"Let me take the baby, and come along to the house," Regina suggested. "You must be tired after carrying Lisabet. She is getting to be heavy."

Sarah gladly let Regina take the baby. "*Ach* (oh), she isn't too heavy," she told her friend. "Anyway, Edna and I took turns." Nevertheless, her arms ached, and she was happy for Regina's help.

Dena Byler was shocked to have the neighbor children show up, complaining of ill treatment from their Maut. She offered the girls chairs and cool drinks of water and then invited them, "Tell me all about it."

Sarah told them of many incidents when Sadie was unkind and impatient. She finished with the episode of the broken bowl.

"I certainly never thought Sadie Zook would be so unfeeling," Dena responded. "Does she know you came here?"

"Oh, *nah* (no)," Sarah whimpered in a frightened tone of voice. "She would give me a *Buckel voll Schlag* (back full of beating) if I would have told her."

"Did your parents know how she mistreated you?"

"They knew some stuff, but not always. I didn't like to tattle and worry Mom. She was so sick. Dad talked to the Maut, and she said she would try to do better. But the first morning Dad and Mom were gone, she started scolding again until our hired man came in the door. Then she was real nice."

"Regina," Dena told her daughter, "go hitch up Queen. We'll go have a talk with Sadie Zook."

"That won't do any good," Sarah objected. "She'll punish me for running away and telling on her."

"We can't let this go on any longer. Maybe we can work out something else."

Sarah doubted that, but what could she do?

Regina quickly hitched the family driving horse to the buggy and drove to the gate, where Dena and the children stood waiting.

There was a lump in Sarah's throat that would not go away. She was fighting hard to keep tears from falling. As they neared the Troyer homestead, they saw and heard the Maut walking around outside the house and calling, "Sarah, Edna, Sarah — Sarah, answer me!" She stopped as she saw the buggy approaching. Her mouth opened in amazement when she discovered it was Mrs. Byler and Regina with the Troyer girls and Lisabet.

"Where did you find them?" Sadie asked.

"They came over to our place."

"But how? How did they come, and what did they want?"

"Is it all right if we come in, and I'll tell you?" Dena replied.

"Ach yah, come in. Regina, you can tie your rig by the corner hitching post." That was a big post at the corner of the yard fence, with one large brass ring to tie a rope. Close to the buggy shed, there also was a large hitching rack, but it was in the outer yard, farther from the house. Three horses could be tethered there.

Sadie seated Dena Byler and her daughter in the spacious kitchen and offered them some water. Taking baby Lisabet from Dena, the Maut directed Sarah, "Go, change the baby. She's wet."

As Sarah left the room, Sadie asked, "Now, what's this all about?"

"Well," replied Dena, "I hardly know how to tell you, but we're both sisters in the same church, and I hope we can talk this out with no hard feelings."

Sadie only nodded.

"The children walked over to our place about seven this morning and —"

"Walked!" the Maut interrupted. "At seven! And they were there all this time! Why, it's almost ten now. I went down to the truck patch before the sun was so warm. I thought they were in the house all the while. Why would they come to your place?"

"That's what is hard for me to tell you," Dena responded.

"I can tell her, Mother," Regina burst forth. "It's because you're so harsh with Sarah. She told me more than once how you scold her for things she can't help. And besides, the mother of these children is sick! Sarah came to stay with us until her folks get back. I don't blame her. How would you like to be yelled at all the time?"

"Regina!" Dena was shocked. Never had she seen her daughter so bold and rude.

"You don't know what it's like," Sadie addressed her accuser. "I want to be patient and treat them better, but almost every day I have these sick headaches. Many times I can hardly see, my head hurts so. But I must work for a living. I have no one to help me."

"Can't the doctor help?" Dena asked gently.

"I've been to so many doctors, and they can't seem to find a cure."

"Why don't you take some time off. I'll speak to the deacon's wife. She may get her husband to see if the church can help you with expenses. You know our people believe in sharing each other's burdens."

"But who would take care of the children and the work here?" Sadie asked.

"I think I can spare Regina until we can make other arrangements." Sarah's heart leapt with joy as she heard this. *Regina — the Maut!*

"You go see Frannie Marner about those headaches. She's good at curing them. Some people call it powwowing, but I call it pressure treatment. She works on pressure points at the back of your neck and the side of the head. It has helped many."

Sarah waited anxiously for the Maut's answer to Dena's suggestion. "Please say yes!" she whispered.

15

The Best News Ever!

One week after Dena Byler's suggestion to Sadie Zook, the switch was made. Regina became a *Maut* (hired girl) for the first time. Sadie had taken the advice Dena offered her. The church agreed to help in whatever way they could. It was decided that Sadie stay on for some extra days to acquaint Regina with the routine and show her where things were kept.

"I've never been a Maut before," Regina said.

"I know," Sadie answered. "Don't worry, you'll learn soon enough." Regina detected a hint of sarcasm in the Maut's answer.

Sarah was a big help in acquainting her friend with household duties.

"I know you and I will get along just fine," Regina told Sarah.

Often singing as she went about her duties, the new Maut brightened everyone's day. Everyone, that is, except Sadie.

"Must you always make that racket while you work?" she asked Regina.

"What racket?"

"*Ach* (oh), that singing."

"Well, it seems to make the work go better. My mom says it gives wings to your feet." She laughed.

"Humph," snorted Sadie. "Does your mother approve of those English songs you sing?"

"She helps sing them sometimes, so I guess she thinks it's okay."

"Such songs like 'Darling Nellie Gray' and 'Letter Edged in Black' — they aren't even in our English hymnals. Don't you sing any of our *Gmeh Lieder* (church songs) in German?"

"Yes, we often do German hymns," Regina assured her.

In two more days, Sadie would be gone. Regina decided to suspend her singing until Sadie left. She would try to do what she could to please her.

Both sets of grandparents were pleased with the change of hired girls and promised to come as often as possible to help along. Sarah wrote to her parents, telling them the news.

Regina had been there three weeks now,

and things were going along quite well. Sadie had started her treatments with Frannie Marner, but it was too soon to tell the results. She reported some relief.

"Read Sarah's letter to me again," Mandy Troyer requested as her husband helped her get comfortable in the recliner.

"Dear Mom and Dad," he began to read, "How are you? Fine, I hope. Mom, I hope you are better. We're all fine. Sadie Zook went home and is going to Frannie Marner because of her headaches. Guess who is working here now? It's Regina Byler. She's nice and doesn't scold us. This is the first time she is a Maut, but you wouldn't know it. She works real good and makes good food, too. I hope we can keep her until you come home.

"*Dawdies* (the grandparents) come often. They take turns on Saturday and Sunday. That's when Regina goes home. *Dawdy* (Grandpa) said he will pay her for working here, and when you come back, you can settle with him. Regina sings a lot and makes us feel better. Oh yes, Lisabet took her first steps yesterday without holding onto anything.

"Edna wants to write, too, so I will close. Do you know yet if we will move out there to Arizona or if you will come back home?

I'll write again, and I hope you'll write soon.

"Good-bye, Sarah.

"P.S. Here is Edna's letter."

"Hello, Mom and Dad. Regina is here. We like her. I want you to come soon. I had a loose tooth, and Grandpa Weaver pulled it out with his *Zangli* (pliers). It didn't hurt much. He gave me a nickel. I put it in the handkerchief drawer until I make up my mind what to buy. From Edna."

Mandy sighed and wiped away a few tears. "*Denk mol von es* (think of it, once)," she moaned. "Our baby took her first step, and I wasn't there to see her. Oh, Sam, our children are growing up so fast! And Regina Byler, she seems too young to look after our family."

"Mom, you must not let yourself get so upset. Everything will work out. It always does. We will leave it in *Gottes Hende* (God's hands). We know his way is best, even though we don't understand. Let's pray as Jesus taught us: '*Dein Wille geschehe auf Erden wie im Himmel* (your will be done on earth as it is in heaven)'."

"Yes," Mandy answered, feeling comforted.

The weeks passed quickly, and soon

111

school would start again. Aunt Salome, both grandmas, and some of the other church women were busy sewing school clothes for the Troyer children. Like Amish people everywhere, they were seeking to follow Bible teaching: If someone is in need and others are able to help, it is a duty and privilege to do so.

Sarah was changing from a young girl to womanhood. She had many troublesome questions and found a true friend in Regina. This Maut did not make fun of her ignorance but was honest and open to hear about her needs. How Regina loved Sarah! But she didn't say just that; in good Amish fashion, she only showed her love by her kindness.

"Sarah, I think the mail just came. Why don't you go and get it, and then we'll finish our baking."

It was Saturday, and Regina was working today as neither grandparents could come. Grandma Weaver had stubbed her bare toe against a stone at the edge of her flower bed, and hurt it badly. She couldn't even wear her shoe. Grandma Troyer had a dentist appointment but said she would come in the evening.

Sarah did not need be told twice to bring in the mail. Almost before Regina had the words out of her mouth, Sarah was out the door. The first thing she always looked for was a letter from Arizona.

"Here it is!" she exclaimed, almost falling over her feet as she stumbled through the kitchen door.

"My goodness, here what is?" Regina laughed, watching the antics of Sarah.

"A letter, a letter from Mom and Dad!" Sarah ripped the envelope open, unfolded the letter, and began reading rapidly.

"Start over and go slower," Edna requested. "I can't make out what you're saying."

"Here, Regina, you read it."

"Well, all right. Simmer down!" The young Maut laughed as she reached for the letter and began to read.

"Dear family. Greetings in Jesus' name. This will be a short letter as I expect we may see you soon. Mother's health seems somewhat better. We think the climate here is helping her. Will come home to make plans. Expect to come around the eighth or ninth of October. Mother wants to come, too, if she is able. I wrote to *Dawdy* Troyers (the Troyer grandparents). They will tell you more. Dad."

Sarah was so happy. "Oh, Regina, they're coming home. I can't wait to tell the boys. May I run out to the barn and tell them? May I?"

"Go on before you burst!" Regina laughed again. Edna also was excited about the news. Who could help it? Sarah's enthusiasm was catching, even if one didn't know what she was happy about.

That was the best news ever!

16

It Can't Be!

Twilight was creeping softly across the Arizona desert. The sun had set in a blaze of glory, and a gentle breeze stirred in the citrus trees by the window.

Mandy Troyer was happy that they had been able to rent this room from Goldie Treen, but now she was ready to go home. Goldie had given them a fair rental price and often brought cookies, cakes, casseroles, and even reading material to share. One of the books she loaned was full of poems. Mandy Troyer loved poetry, and she read a favorite one over and over.

"I'll be so glad to leave this room and move into a bigger place," she told her husband three days before they were planning to leave for Ohio. "It'll be so good to see the children again. But most of all, I want God's will for me."

"*Yah*," Sam replied, "*des is gut* (yes, this is good)."

Mandy picked up the book of poems and turned to her choice one.

"Samuel, I want to read this poem to you. It's just the way I feel, and I want to share it." She began to read:

I do not know, I cannot tell
Just when my Lord may come for me.
But this I know, that all is well
And that his face some day I'll see.
I do not know, I cannot say
When he shall change this house of clay.
But this I know 'ere very long,
I'll hear the call, "Child, come home."
I do not know, but come what may,
The Lord is still my strength and stay.
No matter then what life may bring,
For this I know, the Lord is King.

Mandy laid the book on the stand by her chair and sighed deeply. "I would rather go back home to our church and relatives to live," she told her husband. "But if it is best to move here, well then, God's way is best."

"Yah, *des is waahr* (this is true)," Samuel Troyer agreed.

"We can't bring the *Maut* (hired girl)

along, though," Mandy reminded him.

"Sarah is getting old enough to do more housekeeping," Sam assured his wife.

"She's a good worker, and by the time we have moved she'll be twelve. As my health improves and I'm able to work again, we'll get along real well." A smile appeared on Mandy's face.

"What are you grinning about?" Samuel wondered.

"*Ach* (oh), that Sarah! I remember her telling me that she will be forever eleven. Well, that was a short forever!"

"Just you wait until she's our age," Sam declared. "She'll change her way of thinking. Birthdays come around much faster after thirty."

"What kind of work will you and the boys do out here in Arizona, Sam?" Mother asked. "The boys have never known anything except farming."

"Don't you go worrying about that. Henry is a pretty good painter, and I suppose we could learn the carpenter trade. I've always liked working with tools. You know how Joe is once he gets a hammer in his hand. Remember the bird house he tried to build when he was only five?" Sam laughed.

"I sure do. He didn't do too bad a job if he would have left an opening for the

Veggel (birds) to get in," Mandy observed.

"Oh, don't you know how he figured that out? He said the birds will peck a hole the size to fit them. Then they can go in and out." Sam and Mandy laughed again at the memory of Joe's shenanigans.

Thus the evening passed pleasantly.

"Tomorrow I think I'll go and see about a house I saw advertised in the *Phoenix Sun*. If the rent is reasonable and it suits our needs, I'd like to rent it now. That way when we come back to stay, we'll already have a place."

"Yah, whatever you think is best," Mandy consented.

Goldie Treen came down the sidewalk and stopped by with something for the Troyers. As Samuel answered her knock, she called, "I know it's getting late, but I have a card for you."

"Come in," Sam invited her.

"Hello, Mrs. Troyer. Are you feeling better?"

"Yes, today I felt pretty good. Sit down, won't you?" Mandy invited.

"Oh, no. I must get over to my part of the house. I was down the street visiting Mrs. Tragert. She gave me this card and said it was in her mailbox. It's for you." Goldie handed the card to Mandy.

"Oh, it's from Sarah!" Mandy exclaimed. "I hope everything is all right." Quickly she began to read:

"Dear Mom and Dad. How are you? We're fine. I'm glad you're coming home. Grandpas are helping us get ready to move. I can't wait to see you. Sarah."

"Who is Sarah?" Goldie asked.

"She is our oldest girl and a good child," Mandy told her.

"I believe that, if she's at all like her parents. I sure hate to lose you folks. If my house were only larger, I'd keep your whole family. But one room is hardly big enough for seven. I'll be in and out before you leave."

"Goldie, I'll get the books together that you lent me and give them back tomorrow. There is one poem I would like to copy, if you don't mind."

"Of course I don't mind. Well, I'll see you tomorrow then. Good night."

After Goldie left, Sam stretched to his full height. "Guess it's bedtime. You ready to call it a day, Mandy?"

"I thought after our *Owedgebet* (evening prayer), I would like to copy that poem and maybe write a card for Sarah. She seems to miss us the most."

"Ach, *ich wees net* (I don't know) about

that. I'm sure all our children miss us. Sarah only shows it more. Are you sure you aren't too tired to do all that writing tonight yet?"

"It's something I feel I must do tonight. Tomorrow I may not get to it. I want to copy those words for my children. Don't ask me why, but it's such a strong urge to write them now."

"Whatever you want — only don't tire yourself. We may get home before Sarah gets your card," Samuel teased.

After reading from the prayer book, he said good-night to his wife. "Don't stay up too late," he advised her. "I'll see you in the morning."

As Mandy began writing, Samuel heard her quietly say, "But this I know, that all is well."

First rays of light were peeping at the corners of the window. Samuel sat up with a start. He hadn't slept through the night for a long time. Why, he hadn't heard Mandy cough once. She lay beside him, quiet and relaxed, with just a trace of a smile on her face.

"Mandy," Sam whispered. "Mandy, are you ready to wake up?"

There was no response and no sign of breathing.

Fear clutched at Sam's heart. Gently he touched his wife's cheek. She was no longer warm.

Sam sprang to his feet. "No, it can't be!" he moaned, pacing the floor. "It just can't be!"

But Mandy was gone.

17

Joy and Sorrow

Sarah didn't hear the car come up the drive. She was in the milk house, washing the buckets from the morning's milking. Sarah was singing as she worked, deep in thought and anticipation that her parents would soon be home. The milk house door opened, and Sarah unexpectedly looked into the face of Grandpa Troyer.

"Why, *Dawdy* (Grandpa), I didn't think you were coming till Wednesday. Isn't that the day you and *Mammi* (Grandma) take your turn? But I'm *froh* (glad) you're here. It's only a couple days yet until Mom and Dad come home. Edna asks me all the time how many nights we have to sleep before they get here. Soon she won't need to ask." Sarah laughed.

Grandpa Leroy put his hand on his granddaughter's shoulder. "*Ach* (oh), Sarahlie." He hadn't called her Sarahlie for a long time.

Sarah detected a sadness in his tone of voice. "Dawdy, what's wrong?"

"Come on to the house. We need to talk with you children."

Fear gripped Sarah's heart as she saw Grandpa brush a tear from his cheek. The boys, Edna, and Regina were already seated in the living room, and Grandma Clara was crying.

"What is it?" Sarah asked. "*Was is letz* (what's wrong)?"

"Children," Grandpa began, "I wish we wouldn't need tell you this. Walter Mason got a call from your father this morning. Your mother passed away sometime during the night. Walter brought us over to be with you as soon as we could get away."

Sarah began to scream. "No! No! Mom was better. Dad wrote it in his last letter. He said we would move to Arizona. I don't believe it. There's a mistake. I'll show you myself." She got up and took the envelope from the letter holder. "See!" She handed it to Grandpa.

"Yes, Sarah, I know she seemed better. We don't know what happened. Let us remember, God knows best."

Sarah couldn't understand why this would be best. Well, she would wait and ask her father. Grandma Clara hugged the girls one by one, to show how much she loved them.

Regina came to sit with Sarah. She didn't know what to say to her friend, so she didn't say anything. Yet Sarah sensed Regina's caring, and her frustration gave way to tears.

"When is Dad coming?" Henry asked.

"All I know," replied Grandpa Leroy, "is that he told Walter Mason he'll come as soon as things are taken care of there and arrangements can be made."

Walter entered the living room. "Shall I wait for you?" he wondered.

"No," Grandpa answered. "We'll stay a while."

"I'll be leaving then. But if I get any more information, I'll let you know," Walter promised.

"*Yah* (yes)," Dawdy answered.

Word spread rapidly through the Amish community, and soon the Troyer place was dotted with buggies and several cars. Mandy's parents arrived, and Grandpa Adam helped his distraught wife into the house. Lucy Weaver was weeping profusely.

"Ach, *der aareme Kinner* (you poor children)!" She sobbed. That brought a new flood of tears. Sarah wished she could wake up and find it had only been a dream. But it was painfully real.

Father came home the next evening. Sarah had never seen him so tired. He looked older and so sad.

"What happened, Dad?" Sarah asked.

"I don't know. The doctor said she probably had a relapse."

"What's a relapse?"

"Sarah," Grandma Lucy interrupted, "your dad is tired. Don't ask so many questions."

"It's all right." Samuel waved his hand. "Maybe she needs to talk. Sarah, the sickness came back stronger. All I know is, it was her time to go."

Everything was so different. People were coming and going all the time. As usual for the Amish, they kept the body of the mother and wife in their home.

Many people came to view Mandy Troyer's remains, resting in her coffin made by an Amish carpenter. They offered the family comfort, help, and lots of food. Meals were prepared for the family, relatives, and friends. For a few days, neighbors took over the chores for the bereaved.

Grandpa Troyers needed to go home for a few things before supper. Ervin Martin, a Mennonite neighbor, offered to hitch the horse to the buggy for Grandpa.

"Come on, boys," Ervin invited Henry and Joe. "Maybe you'd better go with me to make sure I get the right outfit." He felt the boys needed to get out of the house for a while. *These children could use a bit of cheering up,* he thought.

While harnessing the horse, he pretended he didn't know how to get the bridle on. The same thing happened when he fastened the belly strap. Watching the boys enjoy his feigned ignorance, he decided to do a really ridiculous thing. Taking the horse to the buggy, he led him into the shafts headfirst.

"No, no!" the boys shouted. "Don't do it like that."

"Oh? Well, then, you show me," Ervin told them.

Henry led the horse out and backed him in between the shafts.

"He can't see which way you tell him to go like that," Ervin protested.

"That's what the lines are for. You guide him."

The boys thought Ervin was the most ignorant fellow they ever saw. After Grandpa Troyers left, the boys told Sarah what Ervin Martin did. Sarah chuckled, distracted for a moment from her grief.

The day of the funeral dawned with a misty rain falling. The gray clouds matched Sarah's mood. She was glad, however, that Regina helped her with her *Schatz un Halsduch* (apron and cape). It was only the second time she wore the outfit, and she was not used to the straight pins. Regina had made the cape dress for her, and Sarah felt grown-up.

"Regina, what will we do without Mom?" Sarah asked.

"I'll stay as long as I can," her friend promised. That was a comfort for Sarah to hear.

The house was crowded. Every room and corner were filled. Five hundred or more attended, not unusual for an Amish funeral. When people arrived after the house was full, they gathered in the buggy shed, cleanly swept for the overflow.

Sarah did not understand much of the preaching. But she did hear the minister say, "Mother's place at the table will be vacant; her rocker will be still. She will need her glasses and her Bible no more."

The grieving girl wanted to shout, *Quit it,* but of course she didn't. Sarah watched her father wipe tears with his big white handkerchief.

Then a Mennonite minister, unknown to

her, stood and said that since some were in attendance who could not understand German, he was asked to say a few words.

"At the request of the bereaved brother, I will read a poem Mandy Troyer copied the night she passed away. She identified with these words." As he read the poem, Samuel lifted his head and nodded.

"What a wonderful testimony," the minister remarked. "Today we feel both joy and sorrow. Joy, because our dear sister no longer suffers this world's afflictions. Sorrow, because she will be missed."

The other ministers nodded in agreement.

18

I Won't! I Won't!

She saw him leaning on the porch railing. Sarah could tell he was crying. Should she go to him or leave him alone? Sarah did not like to see her father cry. It made her cry, too.

It was the morning after her Mother's funeral, and everyone was gone except Regina. Life seemed so dreadfully empty. She turned to go back in the house. Samuel heard her and called her gently to his side. He blew his nose, straightened his shoulders, and said bravely, "Sarahlie." Never before had he called her that. "Sarahlie, we must go on. We will all work together. *Mir kenne's mache* (we can make it)."

Sarah wished she were as confident as Dad seemed to be.

"With God's help, we'll make it," Samuel assured his daughter.

Two months later, after Sunday services,

Sarah heard some startling news. Her friend Katie and she were *botching* (clapping hands) to peas-porridge-hot. Suddenly Katie stopped in the middle of the rhyme: "Did you know that Sadie Zook has a brain tumor?"

"What's a brain tumor?" Sarah asked.

"My mom said it's something that grows on your brain."

"Is it bad, Katie?"

"*Yah, ich denk* (yes, I think). She's going to have an operation."

"But I thought Frannie Marner was treating her," Sarah remarked. "Didn't that help?"

"Mom heard that it seemed to, for a while, but then she started having headaches again."

"You are so *glicklich* (lucky) to have a mom. Regina tells me some things, too, but she has to go home by Christmastime."

"Oh, Sarah, *was duhst du dann* (what will you do then)?" Katie asked.

"Dad said we'll make it. If he said so, we will." Sarah projected an air of determination.

Katie looked at her and wondered how she would feel if she were Sarah.

Sarah certainly was not ready to be a mother at twelve years old. But as

Christmastime approached and Regina prepared to go home, it happened. The duties of housekeeping were pushed upon her more and more. Regina had taught her well, but the responsibilities were not easy.

"Sarahlie," her father said one evening, "since you're still in school and Regina must help at her home by Christmas, we must get another *Maut* (hired girl)."

"Who will we get?" Sarah wondered.

"Well, I heard that Sadie Zook got through her operation real well and is ready to work out again."

"Oh, no, Dad, not her!" Sarah begged.

The boys had been listening to the conversation, and Henry objected also. "*Net die Sadie Zook, die bees aldi Gluck!*" he exclaimed without thinking.

"*Was saagst du* (what did you say)?" Father questioned.

On impulse, Henry had said in Pennsylvania German, "Not Sadie Zook, the angry old cluck (hen)." It was a rhyming verse Sarah and the boys had made up about Sadie.

However, it was unkind and rude. Samuel immediately told his children that he disapproved. "I don't want to hear any more talk like that. We need a Maut, and Sadie is familiar with our household."

The youngsters kept quiet, but Sarah's heart was heavy. She wished she were out of school and could manage the house-keeping.

Sarah lamented to her friend, the current Maut. "Oh, Regina, we children don't want her to come back."

"Maybe she's different now, Sarah. I would stay, if I could, but Mom needs me to help again."

"Can't your older sister, Lena, help her?" Sarah asked.

"Yes, she can, but she has plans of her own."

"Can't she change them?" Sarah asked.

"No, I don't think she would change her plans." Regina smiled because she knew her sister was getting married the first of January, but it was a secret.

Like other engaged Amish couples, her sister and her husband-to-be were keeping things quiet about their upcoming wedding. They derived much joy in playing innocent until two weeks before the marriage would take place. Then the couple would inform the bishop of the church, who publicly would announce it to the congregation.

Sarah could not imagine what plans were more important than letting Regina stay on with their family. It made her sad.

Sunday evening after the chores, Samuel gathered his children to the living room.

"*Kinner* (children), I spoke to Sadie Zook today. She's willing to come back. I hope you will be kind to her as she feels sorry for the way she treated you sometimes — especially you, Sarah. She said she is so ashamed. Sadie says her headaches made her so ill-tempered and *ungeduldich* (impatient). She asked us to forgive her. We must if we want our heavenly Father to forgive us. What do you say, children?"

"But, Dad, what if she doesn't mean it? What if she is snappy to us when you aren't here?" Sarah asked.

"Then you tell me. I'll believe you. She really seems changed. What say we try it?"

The boys and Edna nodded their consent. Sarah only muttered, "I wish Regina would be our Maut forever."

"Forever is longer than we can imagine," Father commented. "You should be careful how you use that word."

Baby Lisabet tugged at Sarah's dress. She was walking well now and followed Sarah constantly. At least, that's how it seemed to Sarah.

"I know, you want me to play with you, Betsy." That was Sarah's pet name for her little sister. "It's about your bedtime, but I will build blocks up with you for a little while." She got the ABC blocks with pictures of farm animals on one side and the alphabet on the other. "Now, don't knock them down before I get them built up." Sarah laughed.

She had only stacked up seven blocks when Lisabet pushed them down. The baby giggled with delight.

"You're such a funny little girl." Sarah hugged her, and they played until Father said to get the baby ready for bed.

"Edna, will you get Lisabet's bottle filled while I wash her up and put her in her nightie?" Sarah asked. The girls worked well together. As Edna appeared in the bedroom with the bottle, she heard laughing.

"Hold still," Sarah directed. "Betsy, you're such a wiggle worm. How can I get you into your nightgown?"

"Do you think Sadie will be good to Lisabet?" Edna asked her sister.

The thought struck terror into Sarah's heart. "She had better be," Sarah answered. "If she isn't, I'll never like her. My mind is made up. I won't, I won't!" she exclaimed.

19
Walking in Another's Shoes

Monday morning came, and with it came Sadie Zook. She appeared thinner, but that was due to her recent surgery.

"Good morning, Sarah," Sadie greeted her. Sarah didn't answer. Sadie could tell at a glance that this wouldn't be easy. Within her heart, she knew why Sarah ignored her. If only she could undo the harm inflicted upon these children by her unkindness — especially to Sarah. It would take time and understanding.

Baby Lisabet stayed close to Sarah's side.

"Lisabet," Sarah said, gently loosening the hand that clutched her dress. "Lisabet, I have to go to school. Here, do something with your *Schpielsache* (playthings)."

Lisabet didn't have many toys, but she did have a *Lumbebopp* (rag doll) she liked. She held to the doll and whimpered as Sarah hurried away.

"Don't worry, Sarah," Sadie called out to her. "Lisabet will be all right. I'll take good care of her. By the time you come home, we'll be friends."

Sarah left with an aching heart. She didn't believe Lisabet would take to Sadie. Sarah had a long day at school. Miss Kinsinger tried to console her distraught student. Sarah poured out her anxieties to her teacher friend.

"You understand, don't you?" Sarah asked.

"I cannot really know what you are going through because I've never been in your situation," Miss Kinsinger counseled. "I hear say Sadie Zook has changed a lot. Some people think she is like a different person. Don't judge her too harshly, Sarah. She must have been suffering a lot of pain before her operation. I'm truly sorry you were so mistreated in the past, but think what it does to you if you hold a grudge. Until we walk in another's shoes, we don't know how we would be."

"But I miss my mom so much, and how can I know for sure that Sadie has changed?"

"Of course you miss your mother. God saw best to call her home. We must not question his ways. Time will tell if Sadie is kind and fair."

Sarah didn't understand why God saw best to take her mother. Wouldn't it have been better if she could have stayed? And as for walking in Sadie's shoes, Sarah didn't want to do that, whatever it meant.

School wasn't much fun anymore since Regina no longer attended. Sarah still had her friends Katie and Lydia, but Regina had been her role model. The day at school dragged on. Sarah could not concentrate on her lessons. When the dismissal bell rang, she was out the door before anyone else.

"Wait, Sarah," called her friend Katie.

"What's your hurry?" her brother Joe asked as he caught up to her.

"I want to find out if Lisabet is all right. Maybe she cried for me all day. I don't like our Maut, and I don't want Lisabet to like her, either," Sarah declared.

Her sister Edna had joined the group of walkers. "Someone has to take care of us, Sarah," Edna reminded her. "Why don't you want to like Sadie? If she's good to us, won't you like her then?"

"No, I won't. She's just acting *freindlich* (friendly) so Dad will give her work. You wait and see. It won't last. How do we know if she takes good care of Lisabet while we're at school?"

"We can soon tell," said Joe.

"How?" Sarah asked. "*Yuscht wie kannscht du saage* (just how can you tell)?"

"Lisabet wouldn't want a thing to do with Sadie if she mistreats her," Henry answered.

"Okay, smarties, wait till we get home. You'll see!" Sarah predicted, quickening her pace.

Sarah burst into the kitchen and found Lisabet happily playing on the floor. She smiled and lifted a string of empty thread spools for Sarah to see. Sadie was taking freshly baked loaves of bread from the oven.

"Umm — *es schmackt gut do hin* (it smells good in here)." Henry sniffed noisily and smacked his lips.

Sarah looked at the new plaything in Lisabet's hands and asked, "Where did she get those?"

"I put them together for her while she was napping," Sadie told her.

Sarah deliberately brought Lisabet's *Lumbebopp* and exchanged it for the string of empty spools. "This is her best toy," she informed the Maut.

Sadie didn't respond, but she could not hide the hurt look in her eyes. Thus began many months of struggles and misunderstanding between Sarah and Sadie Zook. If Sadie folded bath towels lengthwise first, Sarah would undo each one and fold them crosswise.

"That's how we always did them before you came," she cruelly informed Sadie.

"Then I shall try to remember to do them crosswise," the Maut promised.

From time to time Edna and the boys tried to convince Sarah of her ridiculous actions. But she kept them up for over a year.

"Sarah," Edna said one day, "why do you insist on your own way with Sadie? She's trying to make a go of things. You seem to be fighting her all the way. She could tell Dad on you. Did you ever think of that?"

"Just let her tell. Dad told me once he would believe me. Can't you see she's putting on a big front, Edna? I'm surprised at you. I believe she's setting her cap for Dad."

"That's silly. Dad's older than Sadie. It's almost two years now since Mom's gone, and surely if Sadie were still bossy it would have shown up by now. She couldn't pretend this long."

"I don't know how you can be so sure. As for Dad being older than Sadie, well, there's only six years difference."

Sarah even spread some unkind rumors among her friends concerning Sadie Zook.

"Oh, yes," Sarah told Lydia and Katie. "I saw her standing by his chair, poring over a seed catalog. She was telling him what seeds to send for. That isn't all! Sadie even had one hand on his shoulder. I know her plans!"

When this reached the ears of her father, he decided to have a talk with his daughter. "Sarah, what do you mean by telling such stories? Yes, we were looking at the seed catalog. I had asked her a question, and she was only pointing out her suggestions. I've noticed your rudeness to Sadie, and I want it stopped.

"We all know that Sadie was unkind before, but hasn't she proven she's different now? You mustn't hold a grudge. It makes you and those around you miserable. We cannot judge another unless we walk in that person's shoes."

Sarah was silent, turning things over in her mind. Through another year, she was still suspicious of Sadie, but she tried not to let it show.

20

I Was Wrong

No one knew how the house caught fire. They only knew they must move fast, and move they did.

Monday had arrived, and Sadie Zook came with it. She went home on weekends and returned on Monday. As she drove in the lane, soft glows of pink graced the fluffy clouds in the eastern sky.

Father and the boys were already milking the cows. Edna was spending a few days with Grandpa Troyers.

When the *Maut* (hired girl) stepped from her buggy, she saw it. Black smoke was pouring from the attic roof. Without waiting to tie her horse, Sadie ran screaming into the house.

"*Herraus schnell* (get out quick)!" she shouted. "The house is on fire. *Raus, raus* (out, out)!"

Sarah had taken Lisabet from her single

bed to help get her ready for the day. Even though Lisabet was old enough to dress herself, Sarah could do it faster. Besides, any Amish girl wearing a dress with buttons down the back needs help.

"*Fer was grieschet die Maut so laut* (why does the hired girl yell so loudly)?" Lisabet asked Sarah.

"Ach, who knows. She likes to run things, I guess."

Sarah sniffed and paused as she buttoned Lisabet's dress.

"What's wrong, Sarah? Why did you stop?"

"I smell smoke." Sarah opened the door of her room to a hallway filled with smoke. Opening the door gave the fire more air. There was a loud pop, and flames seemed to be everywhere.

Sarah heard Sadie calling through the fiery hall. "Sarah, close the door! Get down on the floor, and crawl to the west window! Hurry! Father and the boys will get you down the ladder. Close the door, Sarah!"

However, Sarah stood as though riveted to the spot. Sadie saw she was motionless. Without any thought for her own safety, Sadie covered her face and dashed through the flames into Sarah's room. Pushing

Sarah aside, she closed the door.

Sarah and Lisabet screamed, "Sadie, your dress is burning!" Sarah cried.

Coughing and choking, Sadie grabbed a blanket from the bed and wrapped it around her burning clothes to choke off the flames.

Father and the boys had the ladder by the west window and were yelling at the top of their voices for the girls to open it and climb down.

When Sam had heard the Maut's first shout, he had run for the house followed by the boys. He had sent the Maut up to get the girls. Noticing the smoke mostly came from the east side, Sam told Sadie not to take unnecessary chances. "If the smoke is too thick, tell the girls to come to the west window. We'll have a ladder ready for them."

Sadie had not expected more than a hallway filled with smoke. She acted quickly when she realized Sarah had panicked. After she smothered the flames on her dress, she pushed Sarah to the window.

"Open the window, Sarah, *schnell* (quick)!"

"Sarah," Lisabet shrieked, "look, the door's starting to burn!"

Sarah looked toward the door, and terror

struck her heart.

"Sarah," Sadie shouted, "my hands are burned. I can't open the window. *You must open the window!*" Sadie gave her a hard shove against the window, and Sarah finally did as she was told. Father and Henry already had the ladder up to the window and told the girls to come on down.

"I'm scared," Lisabet called out.

"Don't be," Father urged. *"Ich kumm und grieg dich* (I'll come and get you)."

Gingerly, Lisabet began her descent as Sarah helped her out the window.

"Now go, Sarah!" Sadie ordered as soon as Lisabet had cleared the first rung.

Trembling with fright, Sarah moved swiftly. Then Sadie started down, trying to hold onto the ladder with her burned hands. About halfway down, Sarah stopped. "My shoes," she called to Sadie, only a few steps above her. "I forgot my shoes."

"Come on, Sarah!" Father yelled. "We can't get your shoes now."

Had it not been for Sadie blocking the way, Sarah might have started back up the ladder. She had no choice but to continue on down.

As soon as the fire was discovered, Father

had told Joe to take his bicycle and ride hard to their English (non-Amish) neighbor's place for help. Mr. Phillips, the neighbor, had called the fire department as soon as he made out what Joe was telling him.

By the time Sarah reached the ground, people seemed to be swarming all over the yard. She saw people carrying out the kitchen stove, table, chairs, the china cupboard, a bed, rockers, the dresser, and armloads of clothing.

In the distance, Sarah heard the wail of a siren. She heard her dad say, "*Dank Gott sie kumme* (thank God they're coming)." She knew he meant the firemen.

The complete upper story was now engulfed in flames, and the men were saying it was no longer safe to enter the house to try to save things.

"Here I am," thought Sarah, "a girl almost sixteen, standing here without my shoes, my hair all *schtrubblich* (uncombed). Just suppose Rudy Kemp is here and sees me like this."

Rudy was a young boy from her church whom several girls admired. She felt a tug at her dress. Lisabet looked up at her with frightened eyes.

"Oh, Lisabet, are you all right?" Sarah asked.

"She's fine, except she's *verschrocke* (scared)," Regina Byler said. Regina and her mother had been trying to comfort Lisabet ever since they arrived. "And how are you, Sarah? Did you get burned at all?" They almost had to shout above the roar of the fire engine, the clanging of the bell, and the shouts of "Move back!"

"No, I didn't get burned," Sarah reported. "But it's a wonder Sadie didn't get burned. Do you know what a dumb thing she did? She ran right through the fire into our room. Her dress was burning, and then she grabbed a blanket and put it around herself."

"Sarah," Regina told her, "Sadie *did* get badly burned. She ran through the fire to save you and Lisabet. Listen, Sarah, if Sadie had not come into that room, you might not have come out. She said you were so frightened that you couldn't move. She pushed you to the window and made you open it and climb down. In her pain, she saw to it that you and Lisabet climbed to safety first. How she must love you!"

Sarah had never experienced what she felt at the moment. "Now I remember! She said she couldn't open the window because her hands were burned. Where is Sadie now?"

146

"Frannie Marner is with her at our place."

"Regina, is she bad off?"

"We don't know yet, Sarah. She says she won't go to the doctor. Frannie will poultice her."

"I must tell her I've been wrong," Sarah groaned. "I didn't give her a chance, but I will now. I want her to know we do need her. Oh, Regina, I was wrong!"

21

A New Beginning

After the fire, Sarah's first meeting with
Sadie was painful for her. Sarah could hardly
speak.

"Oh, Sadie!" She choked, as tears welled
up in her eyes. "I was so wrong. You really
do care about us. Do your burns hurt very
much?"

"Sometimes they hurt, but the main
thing is we are all alive."

"But your arms and hands!" Sarah exclaimed. "Sadie, your face is swollen, and
your hair is singed."

"*Yah* (yes), well, it'll all heal with time.
Frannie Marner poulticed me good with
apple butter, and she refused to let me pay
for it." This was a salve Amish made with
apple butter and other ingredients to apply
to burns, for people or animals.

"I'm sorry for not listening to you,"
Sarah told the *Maut* (hired girl). "From

now on, I'll help all I can."

"Well, I didn't always do my best either," Sadie admitted.

"Maybe we can make a *nie Aafang* (new beginning)," Sarah suggested.

"Yah, *das is gut* (that's good)," Sadie answered.

Arrangements had to be made for the family's lodging after the fire. In spite of the combined efforts of the firemen, friends, and neighbors, the house burned to the ground. It was decided that Samuel Troyer and the boys would stay with Dawdy Troyers. The girls would go with Dawdy Weavers.

"Let Edna and Lisabet stay with Dawdies," Sarah said. "I'm going with Sadie. She needs someone to help her. With her hands burned like that, she can't wash dishes or cook or do hardly anything."

Sadie was touched by this kindness, and it pleased her. Samuel gave his consent, and it was settled.

"We'll help you rebuild, Samuel," the bishop of the church assured him. Many of the onlookers agreed, Amish and non-Amish alike. The Amish way is not to carry insurance but to help supply needs when there is a loss. The women of the community began checking on shoe sizes and gathering material to sew outfits as needed. Some clothing had been salvaged, but much had not.

Sarah was now almost sixteen and would not be returning to school. She would not need any new school dresses, but all her Sunday ones were gone. Father's clothes and the chore coats and boots had been rescued since they were in first-floor closets.

Regina sewed a royal blue dress and a black one, plus a white cape and an apron for Sarah. The royal blue was a bit fancier than her usual garb. Regina had put cuffs on the sleeves. Sarah loved it. She wasn't a member of the church yet, so maybe Father wouldn't object. One evening after Sarah and Sadie had finished supper, Father drove up to the hitching post.

"Dad's here," Sarah observed. "I wonder what he wants. I hope nothing is wrong."

Sadie was almost certain she knew why he had come, but she only said, "Probably wants to talk about the new house."

Sarah ran and opened the door. "*Is ebbes letz* (is something wrong)?"

"*Letz? Nee, nix is letz* (wrong? No, nothing's wrong). I just wanted to see how you two are getting along and plan about the house."

"Well, then, take off your hat and coat and sit a while," Sadie invited.

"How's it going?" Samuel asked as he took a seat in the hickory rocker.

"Real good," Sadie answered.

"Your face isn't as swollen. How are your hands?"

"Better. Frannie comes every day to dress them and change the poultice."

"Oh, Dad," Sarah exclaimed, "you should see them! I can hardly stand to watch. I can tell it hurts, too, every time Frannie takes the loose skin off. I'd do anything if I could change things and make it easier for Sadie. She's so good to me. Why didn't I do as she said so she wouldn't have needed to run through the fire?"

"*Ach* (oh), Sarah, you were too scared to move. You couldn't help it," Sadie tried to comfort her.

"See?" Sarah told her dad. "She doesn't blame me at all. But it was my *Schuld* (fault)."

"Ach, Sarahlie, it was no one's fault. We don't know what caused it. We can't go back and change it, so let's move forward."

Then Samuel looked at Sadie and asked, "Have you told her yet?"

"No," Sadie answered. "Everything has been working out so well for Sarah and me, I guess I didn't want anything to change."

"Why should it change?" Samuel asked.

"Tell me what?" Sarah was puzzled. "I've no idea what you're talking about."

"Sarah, you just said you would do about anything for Sadie, didn't you?" Samuel asked his daughter.

"Yah, and I meant it," Sarah replied.

"Is it all right, then, if Sadie and I get married?"

"Married! You and Sadie! Oh, I don't know what to say. Of course it's all right if Sadie wants to. I'm just so surprised. Do the boys and Edna and Lisabet know?"

"Not yet, but they will soon because we would like to be published after Sadie's burns heal." He and Sadie wanted to keep their marriage plans secret until two weeks before the wedding. Then the bishop would publicly announce it to the congregation.

"Sarah, the frolic for building our new house is set for this coming Tuesday. I would like to talk over some plans with you and Sadie. How many bedrooms do you think we should have? What about a summer house?"

"That's more up to you and Sadie," Sarah suggested. "You two will be living there longer than I will. Edna is doing more and more housework, and soon I'll probably be working as a Maut for others."

"Before we know it, you'll be making *Hochzich* (wedding) plans of your own," Sarah's father teased.

"Oh, Dad!" Sarah gave him a friendly shove.

The evening passed quickly. Soon agreements concerning the house plans were made, and Samuel prepared to leave.

"Now keep our wedding plans under your cap," Samuel told Sarah.

"The secret is safe with me," she promised. Sarah knew it would be hard not to tell Regina, but she knew she mustn't.

Sadie and Sarah sat and talked how things had changed.

"God can bring good out of tragedy," Sadie said.

Sarah thought, *How could I ever dislike this woman?* Sadie could never take the place of Sarah's mother. But they could make a new beginning. And so they would.

"Want to sing a while?" Sadie asked.

"Yes, let's," Sarah answered. They sang hymns from their hearts.

22

Steckelmeedel

A frolic was announced at church to rebuild the Troyer house. In such a work frolic, able-bodied men gathered to erect a house or barn destroyed by fire or storm.

Garner's Construction had dug out the basement and poured the footings for the new house. A few Amish masons had laid up the cement blocks for the basement walls. One morning several neighbors came in and laid the subfloor.

It had been decided the house should have five bedrooms, a large kitchen with pantry attached, a good-sized living room, plenty of closets, a front porch, and a summer house.

The summer house would consist of one large kitchen and a sitting room. It was to be connected to the main house by a breezeway. The family would spend most of their time here during the summer, using only the bedrooms of the large house.

In years to come, as the need presented itself, a *Dawdyhaus* might be built as a separate wing of the farmhouse. But that would only happen when Samuel and his wife could no longer take care of farming or keeping up the large dwelling.

Ten days after the fire, buggies, cars, and vans began to arrive at Samuel Troyer's place. The workers were eager to begin. The man appointed as foreman was barking orders. Everyone took assigned tasks, and work began in earnest.

Women came with well-filled baskets of food. The tool shed had been swept clean, and a three-burner oil stove was put into use.

"Sarah, we need more water to cook these noodles," Dena Byler told her. "It's good your pump didn't burn. At least we can still get good, clear water."

"*Yah* (yes), I'll get some right away." Sarah took the pail. On her way to fetch the water, Sarah was surprised to meet Rudy Kemp.

"Do you know where your dad is?" Rudy asked.

"He had to go after some more roofing shingles. The company didn't send enough. He should soon be back."

"The men wanted to know if he wants the stairway going from the kitchen to the upstairs or from the living room."

"I don't know," answered Sarah, blushing shyly. "Why don't you ask Sadie Zook? She might know."

"What does she have to do with it?" Rudy asked.

"She's going to be . . . my . . . Oh, my!" Sarah caught herself just in time.

"She's going to be what?" Rudy wondered.

"I mean, she's going to be our *Maut* (hired girl) yet. Anyway, Sadie might know."

Rudy was the foreman's son and therefore had been sent to inquire about this matter. He made his way among the chattering, bustling women until he found Sadie Zook. Due to her injured hands, she was only able to observe and entertain some young children.

"Sarah said you might know from which room Sam wants the stairway to lead upstairs," Rudy stated.

"Why, yes," Sadie answered. "I heard him say it should be from the kitchen."

Rudy returned with that information to his father. He was glad Sam Troyer had not been available, so he could talk to his daughter instead. *That Sarah,* he thought, *she's a pretty nice-looking girl. Wonder if she's about ready for* Rumschpringe (going out with the young folks). *Maybe someday I can take her home from the singings.*

On Sunday evenings the youth would gather at a home for singing hymns. Afterward, a boy might offer to take a girl to her home in the dark. It was their social life, often leading from friendship to lasting relationships.

"Rudy, get busy and help with those trusses," his father directed. "Ever since you came back from finding out about the stairway, you've been slacking on the job. You have to do your share or work while we eat," his dad teased.

Rudy snapped to it. He was glad his father couldn't read his thoughts.

Sarah carried pail after pail of water. She helped set up a few makeshift tables. Their good dining table and chairs along with some other furniture salvaged from the fire had been stored at one end of the shed. It was covered with a large tarp. Now the table and chairs were brought out and put to use.

At noon the work stopped. After they washed up, the bishop said, "*Mir welle bede*

157

(let's pray)." The men all removed their hats and caps, and a time of silent prayer followed. Then they all turned to food, fellowship, and fun.

Sarah loved the good-natured bantering which took place. She heard one of the men say, "Hey, Sam, I believe we would get your house done quicker if we would take an hour's nap under a shade tree. It would refresh us!" Many sat on the ground to eat, so this fellow sprawled out, folding his arms, closing his eyes in mock sleep.

"Oh," joked Sam, "we have a better way to refresh you." With that remark, he took a dipper of cold water from the nearby pail and drenched the joker. Sputtering and surprised, the sleepfaker sat up. The crowd broke out in laughter, and soon work began once more.

"Dad," Sarah asked, "can we move home tomorrow? The men are putting the roof on, so we would stay warm and dry."

"The house has been built in a hurry, and I'm pleased, but we can't move in yet. We have a lot of finish work to do."

"What's finish work?" Sarah asked.

"Oh, painting, varnishing, putting cupboards and countertops in."

Sarah didn't even know what countertops were. In their old house, they only had one cupboard. It was a piece of furniture with a bin for flour and one for sugar. Instead of countertops, they had a dry sink. Both the cupboard and sink had storage space for dishes and silverware.

"How long will it be, Dad? I like Sadie, but I miss Lisabet, Edna, and the boys."

"I know. I don't like the family separated like this, either. My plans are for two or three more weeks. We must make the best of it."

Sarah thought the weeks wouldn't end. Some of the relatives and a few women from the church helped with the varnishing and painting. It took longer than Sam anticipated, but one month and four days after the fire, the family moved in.

People from the community were quite generous. Some contributed an extra bed, others a dresser, nightstand, cedar chest, or lots of bedding, which they gave gladly. Sarah had a bedroom all to herself. Edna and Lisabet shared a room, but Henry and Joe had their own bedrooms.

"It's nicer than before the fire," Sarah observed.

"We mustn't be proud," Father told her. "But we must be thankful."

Sarah *was* thankful. Sadie's burns healed well. She was able to do her own work. It was thought best that she remain at her house until after the wedding.

"I must get my dress ready," she told Sarah. They had gone to town earlier and purchased the blue material and white organdy for Sadie's wedding outfit. "You will be my *Steckelmeedel* (decoy girl)," Sadie had teased. "In case anyone suspects something, we can hide the fact by pretending it's for you."

"I've never been a *Steckelmeedel* before," laughed Sarah, "but secrets are fun."

23

Seventeen and a Maut

Sarah and her siblings could hardly hide their excitement. It was Sunday morning, and Father told them this was the day he and Sadie would be published.

"Now, don't tell anyone," Sam warned them. He instructed them to be ready to leave as soon as services were dismissed.

"But aren't we staying for the *Gmehesse* (church meal)?" Sarah inquired.

"No," Sam declared. "I want to leave right away. I'll get enough ribbing without standing around after church."

"*Yah* (yes), but Dad, I didn't plan anything for dinner at home," Sarah objected.

"You don't need to worry. We aren't going home," her dad told her.

"*Wo gehne mir* (where are we going)?"

"Well, Sarah, we're going to Sadie's for dinner. She is not coming to church and invited us over."

This conversation took place at the breakfast table, and the other children began to ask questions also.

"Dad," Edna wondered, "who'll live in Sadie's house?"

"Sadie rents that house. It'll be up to the people who own it to find others to move in."

"Dad, if you marry Sadie," asked Lisabet, now six, "will Sadie be our *Mamm* (mom)?"

"She'll be your *Schtiefmammi* (stepmother)."

Sarah felt rather strange upon hearing those words.

"Our surrey is full with the six of us," Joe remarked. "How will we fit one more in?"

Sam laughed at this. "Where there's a will, there's a way, Joe. Remember, Sadie has a horse and buggy which she intends to keep. I guess maybe you boys and Sarah could drive that rig. Sadie and I already thought of that."

Sarah wondered if there was anything they hadn't discussed. It seemed as if they were making all the decisions. For a moment she felt a pang of resentment. Then she remembered Sadie's sacrifice for her in the fire.

"Girls, get the dishes done up and get

ready. We don't want to be late for church." Sam was one of the *Vorsinger* (song leaders), and he liked to be on time.

"One more question," Sarah ventured. "Are you and Sadie having a big wedding?"

"No," her dad replied. "Sadie and I will be married at our regular church service, two weeks from today. Neither one of us wanted a big fuss and all the work preparing for the usual weddings."

Sarah was glad about that. She dreaded all the cleaning and food preparation it would have involved.

As they rode along the country road to church, the three sisters talked excitedly of the day's events. Sarah had mixed feelings. She liked Sadie, but it was hard to think of her as a stepmother. Would she make all the decisions? Did she expect to be called Mom?

Lisabet seem delighted. "We'll have a real mom," she joyfully exclaimed. She didn't remember her birth mother, who had died when she was a baby. Edna remembered, but she, too, was rather pleased.

"Don't forget," Sam reminded his children as he pulled up to the gate to let the girls step out from the back seat of the carriage. "I'll go out just before the last song, and, girls, you'll be waiting by the gate."

It was hard for Sarah to act natural. She hoped she and her sisters would get to sit at the end of the bench. That would make it easier for them to leave without much commotion.

"You go first," her friends Katie and Lydia urged her. It was the polite thing to do when it was time to enter the room and find your place. Church services were held every two weeks in an Amish home. Backless benches served as pews.

"No," Sarah insisted. "Today Lisabet, Edna, and I want to sit together. I'd rather sit at the end in case I need to take Lisabet to the *Heisli* (outhouse)."

Since Lisabet was old enough to go alone, the girls looked askance at Sarah but didn't question her.

The singing and sermon seemed to drag on and on. Edna and Lisabet did not yet understand much of what was said. They *rutsched* (squirmed), and Sarah nudged them gently. She kept her eyes on Father. As he and the boys left the room, she whispered to Edna, "Now!" and they made their exit. People, especially the women, looked at one another knowingly and smiled. After dismissal, the chattering began.

"I suspected something was up when Sadie wasn't in church today," claimed Dena Byler.

"Yes, and the girls never sat together before," Annie Chupp remarked.

"I figured when Sam built a bigger house, he had something like this in mind," Verba Raber told them. And so it went. Everyone was having a good time sharing their hunches.

Two weeks later the marriage took place in a Sunday morning service as planned. The bishop called Sam and Sadie forward to exchange their vows, and then they took their seats among the other worshipers. Sadie sat among the women, and Sam with the men.

If they had been younger and it were a first marriage, the couple, the bridesmaids, and the groomsmen would have sat on chairs facing each other near the ministers. They would have picked a Tuesday or Thursday and stayed together throughout the wedding service. However, Sam said that in this case, they needed no groomsmen or *Newehocker* (bridesmaids) since the entire congregation served as their witnesses.

That evening both sets of grandparents and Sadie's only brother gathered at the

Troyer's new home for a meal and singing. Sarah heard her grandpa Troyer say to her dad, "I believe she'll make a good mother for the children and a good wife for you."

"*Yah*," Samuel answered, "*ich bin dankbar* (I'm thankful)."

In the weeks and months that followed, things did not always run smoothly. As in any family, there were disagreements. But Sarah and Sadie both learned to talk things out and not let bad feelings fester.

Things changed almost a year after Sadie came to live with the Troyer family as their stepmother.

"Sarah," Sadie reported one day, "Noah Fanny needs a *Maut* (hired girl). She asked me if I think you would be ready to work for others if I can spare you. What do you think?"

Sarah knew Noah Raber's wife, Fanny, and quickly replied, "Yes, I'd like to try it if you can get along without me here."

"That's no problem. Edna can do more household chores."

"How soon does she need me?" Sarah asked.

"You could start anytime."

So that's how it began. Eventually, Sarah helped in many other homes, too.

"I'm going to be a Maut," she told her

friends Katie and Lydia. "I'm almost seventeen and a Maut!"

Sarah was embarking on a new adventure. Remembering her early years, she vowed to be the best Maut ever!

24
The Keyhole

Sarah was now well into her *Rumschpringe* (going out with the young people) years. She enjoyed going to young folks' singings, cornhuskings, box socials, and other gatherings. It was fun to have so many friends, but most of all she enjoyed the company of Mahlon Mast.

Everyone somehow seemed to take for granted that Sarah and Rudy Kemp were meant for each other. They had been seen together after several singings. But when Sarah and Mahlon began keeping company, Sarah somehow knew Rudy was not the one.

"*Wie viel Hatzlin verbrechst du eb du schliesst* (how many little hearts are you going to break before you make up your mind)?" her brother Henry teased.

Sarah made a face at him. "None of your business, *Rotkopp* (redhead)."

Henry had a head full of copper-colored hair. Although many Amish girls admired it, to Henry it was a thorn in the flesh. He didn't know of any other boy with hair the color of his.

On weekends Sarah came home from her *Maut* (hired girl) jobs. The whole family looked forward to these times. Lisabet would beg to sleep with her big sister and was elated when she was allowed to do so.

Sarah brought news from the families for whom she worked. She would also catch up on the week's activities at home. Sometimes the things Sarah told were sad, even tragic. Some were everyday stories, and some were humorous. One Saturday evening as they ate supper together, she related such a happening.

"Let me tell you what Abe's little Susie did this week." Abe Koblentz and his wife, Alma, had a family of eight children. The oldest child was nine. Mrs. Koblentz sometimes felt the need to have a few minutes of quiet away from the children.

"Alma told me she would go bring the cows in from the pasture since she needed a little time alone. While she was gone, a salesman came, and Susie was out in the yard. He asked if her mother was home.

Susie is only six and doesn't know English too well yet. 'No,' she answered, 'Mom went down the keyhole.' "

How everyone laughed! Edna, who was taking a drink of water at the time, sprayed water everywhere. She almost choked. Just to picture this was hilarious, for Alma Koblentz was not a small woman.

"Did the salesman wait to see this woman who could fit through a keyhole?" Henry asked.

"Yes, and if so, did he ask to see the keyhole?" laughed Joe.

They all knew that little Susie spoke the best she knew, combining languages. In Pennsylvania German *cows* are called *Kieh*, pronounced "key"; and to bring them in is to *hole* them.

"We must not make fun of Alma Koblentz," Samuel told his family.

"Oh, we aren't," the children assured him. "It's just so funny what Susie said."

"Yeah, but Dad, don't you find it amusing to picture it?"

Sam chuckled and admitted it seemed absurd. "But let's not get carried away with our laughter."

When things quieted down, Sarah stated, "Well, I have something to tell you, and I'm very serious about it. Dad, Mom, I am starting instruction for baptism."

It was the first time Sarah had called Sadie "Mom." Sarah didn't realize she had used the word, but Sadie noticed, and her heart was thrilled. She had a twofold reason to rejoice: because it seemed so natural, with the rest of the family calling Sadie "Mother"; and because Sarah was deep in thought about her baptism.

"Why, you called Sadie 'Mom'!" Lisabet exclaimed.

"Did I? Well, it sounds good to me if you don't mind," Sarah told Sadie.

"Of course I don't. I always hoped you would."

"I'll need a new *Daaffrack* (baptismal dress)," Sarah commented. "Will you help me pick a good material, Mom?"

"If you want," Sadie answered. Now she had no more doubt that she was accepted for sure.

Sunday morning arrived. The congregation kept singing as usual when the ministers withdrew for their counseling session. Seven eager young folks followed them to begin instruction in preparation for baptism and church membership.

Mahlon Mast was not in the instruction class. People had speculated that if Sarah would join the church, so would Mahlon.

171

Then they might be published to be married.

"What's Mahlon dragging his feet for?" Henry teased. "Is he starting late just to throw us off track?"

"A girl can't marry if she isn't asked," Sarah informed him.

"Hey, Mahlon," the boys badgered him, "what's the holdup? Who are you trying to trick? We bet you'll be an old *Gheiertmann* (married man) by fall!"

However, Mahlon laughed off the comments. "A boy can't marry until the girl takes a notion."

Unknown to everyone, Sarah and Mahlon had been making plans. He would join the fall group of candidates for baptism and be married in the winter.

"That will give us time to get all the harvesting done, and my folks will be ready to move into the *Dawdyhaus* (grandparents' wing of the farmhouse)," he told Sarah. "It's not that they're too old to stay in the large house, but ever since Mother broke her hip and had that back injury in the car-buggy wreck, she can't keep up with the work."

"I understand," Sarah responded.

"Do you mind living so close to my folks?" Mahlon asked. "You may need to help Mom a lot."

"I shall not mind a bit," Sarah assured him. "Your family will become my family."

Mahlon silently thanked God for such an understanding girl, who was echoing the commitment of the biblical Ruth: "Your people shall be my people."

Sarah needed to tell Sadie of her marriage plans for January first, the date chosen by Mahlon and herself. She knew she needed to put up fruits and vegetables, make apple butter, quilts, and a comforter or two.

"Mom," Sarah said one Sunday afternoon. "Mom, I need to talk to you while we have a few minutes to ourselves. Can you keep a secret? *Ach* (oh), of course you can. I know I can trust you."

"What are you talking about?" Sadie wondered.

"I need to do some canning and quilting before winter."

"*Was saagst du* (what are you saying)? Does this mean what I think?"

"Yes, Mahlon and I plan to get married on New Year's Day."

"But he isn't a church member yet."

"He will be. Mahlon is joining in the fall."

"We'll get busy right away," Sadie declared. "Don't worry; your secret is safe with me."

"I'll tell Dad tonight, too, but I know he won't say a word," Sarah added.

She took most of the summer to stay home and help with the extra work. People thought it was in preparation for baptism and helping to get ready for church services held at their home twice that season. The quilting they had was supposedly for Sadie, and no one was the wiser.

Sarah was baptized at a service in her own home. She was surrounded by family and friends, the love of her future husband, and God's love. What more could she ask for?

25

This I Know

Sarah was busily sorting through her belongings. Summer was over, and autumn was already yielding to the chill of winter. Mahlon Mast was now to become a member of the church, and soon they would be married.

As Sarah cleaned out her top dresser drawer, a piece of paper slipped from between some hankies and floated to the floor. She retrieved it and began to read. A gasp escaped her lips.

"What's that you've got?" asked Lisabet, who had just entered the room.

"Why, it's the English poem read at Mother's funeral. I forgot I had it."

"Where did it come from?"

"I must have kept it underneath my good hankies, which were gifts. I never use them, except for special."

"Well, I don't remember the poem," Lisabet said. "May I see it?"

"Sure." Sarah handed her the piece of paper. Sarah was glad Lisabet didn't ask her to read it to her. After these many years, Sarah still choked up as she reread those words.

"This is so *scheene* (nice)," Lisabet commented as she finished reading. "But why are you going through all your stuff?"

"*Ach* (oh), Lisabet, you are a *schnuppich Katz* (snoopy cat). We all need to straighten up drawers and do away with what we don't need anymore. Here, let me see if my black head coverings fit you. Hold still." She placed the cap on Lisabet's head.

"Oh, Sarah, it's way too big." Lisabet laughed. "Why don't you want them anymore?"

"I'm keeping one," Sarah answered. "I don't need more. Oh yes, I'll keep my good one for Sundays. Maybe Edna can use my others."

She was not about to tell Lisabet that soon she would be wearing a white covering as a married woman.

Driving home from singing one Sunday evening, Mahlon suggested, "Sarah, I'd like for you to come have dinner at my place on Thursday. The rest of the family will be there. It's Thanksgiving, and I hope you can come. You don't have other plans, do you?"

"No, I don't, but wouldn't that be too much for your Mom? You told me she hasn't been well since the accident."

"Oh, don't worry. My sister and family from Wisconsin will be here, and they'll see to the meal and everything. My brothers' wives always pitch in and help, too."

Mahlon Mast only had one sister, and she lived so far from home. Her husband owned and operated a large sawmill, and their visits to Ohio were few.

"I'd like for you to meet my family. You'll come, won't you?"

"All right," Sarah promised. "I'll come." Then, as an afterthought, she confided, "But I'll be nervous!"

Mahlon laughed. "What's to be nervous about? They'll all like you."

"I hope so."

"Everything will work out fine," Mahlon assured her.

"What do you mean?" Sarah asked, bewildered.

"My sister and family are staying until after New Year's. So they'll help my parents move into the small house and also be here for our wedding on New Year's Day. Sarah, I had to tell them about the wedding. I hope you don't mind. They had to know who was moving into the large house."

"I understand," Sarah responded. "There were too many changes being made not to have questions."

"They won't let the cat out of the bag," Mahlon told Sarah.

It was of great importance for Amish couples to keep marriage plans secret. Many people, however, were saying that because Mahlon Mast was now a church member, there would soon be a wedding for Sarah Troyer and him.

Sarah did have Thanksgiving dinner with the Mast family. Her nervousness soon left her, and she felt at home. It pained her to see the effort it took for Mrs. Mast to do simple tasks.

"I know I'll enjoy helping her," Sarah told Mahlon later. "She's so frail and kind. Why, she made me feel like one of the family right away."

"And soon you shall be," Mahlon replied. "Yes, my mother is a kind-hearted person. She always puts us first. I just don't understand why that accident happened and left her so crippled. We never hear her complain although we know she is in almost constant pain."

"I guess some things in this world we never will understand," Sarah agreed. "Like when my mother died, leaving young children behind. Or why we lost our home to a fire. We never knew what caused it. Nor why our *Maut* (hired girl), now my stepmother, was burned in that fire when I panicked. Ach, listen to me," Sarah interrupted herself. "Those things are all in the past. You would think I'm not thankful for all the good things in my life. Do I sound ungrateful?"

"No," Mahlon decided. "You're human, as are we all. We have unanswered questions, but someday we will know why. God's ways and thoughts are far above ours."

"Yes," Sarah agreed, "and God's way is best."

One evening in December, Sadie said, "Sarah, I want to give you a nice wedding. Is there anything special you would like?"

"Oh, *Mamm* (Mom)," Sarah answered, "you've been so good to me, in spite of how I treated you when you came back as our Maut after your operation. I'll be satisfied with an ordinary wedding. Don't go to extra bother."

"If we want to count the unkind things we used to do, I believe you remember how it was *before* my surgery. I must have been impossible."

"Listen to us," Sarah observed. "Let's just be happy for how it all turned out."

Sadie really did want to do something special for this young woman she had learned to love. She had a sudden inspiration. Sarah had told her that the Bible her mother left her was falling apart. She wanted to keep it because it had been her mom's. This gave Sadie an idea. If she couldn't give her a large wedding celebration, she would at least give her a special gift.

January first was a beautiful day. The sun shone on a blanket of new-fallen snow. Mahlon looked handsome in his new black suit and his well-trimmed beard. Sarah was the picture of a blushing young bride in her new blue dress with white cape and apron. Soon she would lay aside her black head covering and wear the white one.

The bishop was speaking forcefully about the binding of the marriage vows. He and all the Amish listeners were certain that marriage was for life, "until death do us part."

"How much grief could be spared," the preacher asked, "if this were the law of the land?"

The vows were exchanged, and then the bride and groom, along with the wedding party, were on their way to the Troyer home for the noon meal and fellowship. As the happy couple opened their gifts, there was one different from all the rest.

"Hey, Mahlon, how many towels did you get?" Mike Weisel asked.

"Never mind," Mahlon answered.

Some claim you will have a child for each towel among the wedding presents.

"You'd better count," joked Harvey Lapp. "Got to make sure you have enough beans to feed them."

Sarah laughed, but when she opened Sadie's gift, her eyes filled with tears of gratitude. It was her mother's Bible, which had been rebound. Along with the Bible was a small cross-stitched wall hanging of her Mother's favorite poem.

"What is it?" Mahlon asked.

Sarah couldn't speak. She showed him the poem and the signature. It read: "God bless you. From your two Moms."

Mahlon closed the Bible and handed it back to his wife. He gently squeezed her hand to let her know he understood.

If there was ever any doubt in Sarah's mind about Sadie, it was surely gone. She turned to Mahlon and declared, "*Ich hab die bescht Schtiefmammi in die Welt* (I have the best stepmother in the world). This I know, she must really care, or she wouldn't have done such a nice thing for me."

Like her mother, she knew that all was well.

The Author

Raised in the fertile farming community of Plain City, Ohio, Mary Christner Borntrager was seventh in an Amish family of ten children. In her series, Ellie's People, she depicts the Amish way of life in which she was raised.

At the age of nineteen, she married John Borntrager. Their family consisted of two boys and two girls. Now she is grandmother to eleven persons and great-grandmother to four children.

Mary's education began with eight grades of elementary school. After leaving the Amish, she attended teacher-training institute at Eastern Mennonite College (now University), Harrisonburg, Virginia. For seven years she taught in a Christian day school. After she and her husband earned certificates in youth social work from the University of Wisconsin, they cared for emotionally disturbed and neglected youth.

Borntrager is a member of the Ohioana Library Association and the author of eight novels in the Ellie's People Series. Because of reader interest, she is kept busy with public speaking and autographing sessions. Mary was interviewed on local TV and radio and receives many warm letters from her fans.

In 1994 Mary wrote a play based on her first novel, *Ellie*. It was presented to appreciative audiences at Hartville (Ohio) Mennonite Church, where she has been a member for forty years.

Mary's husband passed away just before her first book was published. She lives in North Canton, Ohio, with a granddaughter. Her hobbies include writing poetry, reading, quilting, memorizing the Bible, playing table games, and embroidering. She enjoys family reunions and get-togethers with her children and their families.

Borntrager is thankful for her Christian heritage and wants to pass it on. She hopes her series, Ellie's People, will bring pleasure to many readers and a better understanding of the Amish and their way of living.